Six-Gun Fury

Six-Gun Fury

Jackson Cole

WHEELER
CHIVERS

This Large Print edition is published by Wheeler Publishing, Waterville, Maine, USA and by BBC Audiobooks Ltd, Bath, England.
Wheeler Publishing, a part of Gale, Cengage Learning.

LIBRARY OF CONGRESS CATALOGING-IN-PUBLICATION DATA

Cole, Jackson.
    Six-gun fury / by Jackson Cole.
        p. cm. — (Wheeler Publishing large print western)
    ISBN-13: 978-1-59722-746-9 (pbk. : lg. print : alk. paper)
    ISBN-10: 1-59722-746-3 (pbk : lg. print : alk. paper)
    1. Large type books. I. Title.
PS3505.O2685S58 2008
813'.52—dc22   2008003706

BRITISH LIBRARY CATALOGUING-IN-PUBLICATION DATA AVAILABLE

Published in 2008 in the U.S. by arrangement with Golden West Literary Agency.
Published in 2008 in the U.K. by arrangement with Golden West Literary Agency.

U.K. Hardcover: 978 1 405 64586 7 (Chivers Large Print)
U.K. Softcover: 978 1 405 64587 4 (Camden Large Print)

Printed in the United States of America
1 2 3 4 5 6 7 12 11 10 09 08

Six-Gun Fury

Chapter I
Colt's Ambush

For countless miles the gray wilderness rose from the valley of the Pecos, river of death. East was Horsehead Crossing, dreaded by men, one of the few fords over the deep black canyon where Comanches and Kiowas took the blood toll. Feeder creeks reached the main stream through other deep canyons, for the most part inaccessible to men save by rope. Above, the tableland was dense with chaparral. Over all that panting, weary grayness of dust, rose the weird forms of giant cacti and tortured rocks.

This, across the Pecos, was a natural hell, arid and malignantly cruel. Nature appeared to have vented all her bad temper in this immense space. The men who rode the winding, dark trails were cruel. Even the long-horned steers that ran the brakes seemed unusually savage, ready to attack and gore intruders.

West of the fearsome river canyon was no-man's land.

But there are ever men who go where others dare not — hardy pioneers whose blood eggs them on to dare death in any form. Some went for sheer adventure, others to wrest from nature the first of primitive wealth. To prey on them came the lawless, the raiders and killers overbold, because no check on them existed.

A bad-tempered, whining wind whipped up the gritty dust, rustling the dry pods of the mesquite and the fronds of other aromatic plants, greasewood and sage. This wind seemed determined to blind and choke the riders descending from the western mountains.

The vastness of the country made them appear like tiny ants crawling on a wide expanse of floor, avoiding the worst of rocks and rough spots. There were about fifteen horsemen. They rode with heads bent into the wind, bandannas drawn up, to sift out some of the grit from the air they must breathe. They were not cowmen, for they wore heavy corduroys, thick leather jackets, sweated Stetsons and most had high laced boots. But all carried pistols, ammunition belts, and rifles in slings ready for use.

First came the leader of the train, horse

with nose down, laboring against the murderous wind. Then two more riders followed, and half a dozen pack mules plodded on without appearing to notice the dust. Flankers stayed on both sides of the mules, whose loads were covered with thick canvas tied on with strong ropes. More men rode in the drag.

The trail they were following eastward, back toward far-off civilization, had climbed the top of a ridgy mountain, winding in and out among scrub pines and bush to the bottom. The ravine was dry. The stones showed that in the occasional cloudbursts it was a raging torrent, helping further to erode the earth.

The sun was still up, but it was a dull brass globe through that haze of alkali. The air was baking hot, for the wind was an oven breath.

"Waterhole beyond that cut, boys," bawled the caravan leader, waving back. "We'll camp once we're through."

The wind whipped his voice on. Men who missed the words understood his gesture and were glad. Night would fall like a sudden blanket thrown over their heads. And if the wind kept on, they might be lost within a few hundred yards of their goal.

The mules quickened their pace, scenting the water before the horses did. Their huge ears shot forward with eagerness.

The caravan leader shoved down a shale-covered slope. He put his horse through the cut that wound in and out among high boulders covered with a gray-green lichen that scaled off at a touch.

To south and north lay veritable hells of spewed boulders and sharp buttes. Only here and there could any plants find a roothold. But the narrow cut, for a quarter mile, took the trail through this impasse.

Now the line of animals and men was fully inside the pass. In the west, the brassy sunball was huge and reddening to blood color. Heads down in weariness and away from the dust whipping through the cut in forced draught, the riders did not see the line of rifles that stuck out from the rocks over them.

Up at the west end the giant leader, Stetson strapped tight over carrotty hair, eyes narrowed to red slits above the bandanna edge, dropped a burly, leather-covered arm. It was the signal to fire.

A murderous volley roared from deadly rifles, aimed a few yards above the unsuspecting victims. The long line of Winchesters and Sharps flashed fire and slugs.

Traveling such a short distance, the bullets could not miss. They tore into the heads and chests of the horsemen plodding through the gap. Blood spurted from riven arteries and smashed brainpans. Frightened steeds reared, whinnying and screaming. The mules bucked, tried to turn and run for it. But there were riders awaiting them as they came out at both ends of the trap.

A tall, thin devil in leather and spurred boots, double cartridge belts crossing his lean shoulders, shouted over the whining wind. He was masked and wore a wide sand-colored Stetson.

"Get them packs off, pronto!" he yelled.

The men with him were masked, too. They were evidently trained gunfighters. From what could be seen of their faces, hard and smoky-eyed, no pity showed for those they had just slaughtered. The mules, roped or seized by bridles, were hurriedly freed of heavy packs, turned loose. The canvas loads were fastened with diamond hitches to ready horses.

The whole deal, run through with cold-blooded efficiency, took only about twenty minutes. Then the chief of the murderers, walking his tall gray mustang through the cut, signaled his hombres.

They started back west. As the chief's gray

swung, the brand could be seen on the mustang's thigh — a bar and a C after it.

In the darkening sky, black specks swooped down on the death cut. From other points, miles away, more vultures saw the descent of their fellows. On great wings they hurried to the spot. A coyote set up a blood howl that echoed eerily through the Pecos wilderness.

It was days later when another party of men came from the west, hunting the caravan. Only picked skeletons remained of what had been men and animals. The clothing had been pulled to shreds by raucous scavengers.

A large man, wearing what would have been a black suit but for the covering dust layers, stared in horror as his horse stopped short, shying from the grim piles of bones. He turned his broad face back, eyes widening.

"Here they are — dead!"

A huge, sloppy fellow with a bulbous red nose and broken veins in his cheeks, thick-lipped mouth open, spurred forward to stare at the remains.

"Gawd!" His eyes, enflamed by whiskey, grew narrow. "Hey, Roberts, looka this!" The man called Roberts was about fifty, a man with a newly tanned skin, and a care-worn brow.

"Horrible, horrible," he gasped, as he came up beside the other two. "All dead, Morse!"

"Yeah, all of 'em, shot down with no chance at all," the sloppy hombre, Ted Morse, snarled. "They've got our gold, thirty thousand dollars wuth. Killed our friends — I won't stand any more of this, Roberts. See, Potter? This is what I told yuh. It's the third raid on my trains!"

Ted Morse, manager of the Pecos Lady mine, was beside himself with rage against the killers. He raved and ranted as he strode up and down, looking at the evidence.

"Ambushed — No chance at all — But wait. Here's a horse that ain't ours, gents."

George Potter and David Roberts hurried to him. Morse pointed at the torn hide of a long-dead mustang.

"Kin read that brand, Bar C. The ranchers did it. I knew it all along. I told both of you so! They're sore 'cause we've roiled their creek and spoiled their winter range in the hills. Carlton's the boss of 'em. They mean to chase us out of the mountains."

"I'm afraid you're right, Morse," Roberts agreed. He shook his head sadly. "This'll be a terrible blow to the people back home. After the glowing reports I sent them about the Pecos Lady mine, it's agonizing to run into trouble like this. Potter, you'll have to ride to the telegraph office as soon as possible and wire Mr. Elms in Austin. You were sent here to find-out what was going on, and you've found it!"

"I'll get 'em. I'll get even with those dirty cowmen!" shouted Ted Morse. "No law west of the Pecos except gun law, they say. Well, they'll get what they've asked for. From now on I'm givin' 'em two bullets for one."

With the three leaders were two dozen sturdy miners, laborers hired to work the Pecos Lady. The mine was so far from civilization that without rails it was not profitable to ship ore. The gold was extracted by sluices at the spot, and shipped in bullion and bags to the outer world.

The faces of the miners were dark with anger as they looked on the remains of their comrades, slaughtered here in the cut. Honest, hard-working fellows, they were yet men of action who would fight for their rights.

"Sheriff ought to be told," Potter suggested.

"Sheriff!" snapped Ted Morse. "Why, the hull country could be slaughtered and that blind fool would never catch a fly!"

"It's a mighty big territory he's supposed to cover," Potter objected. "I'll speak to him when I hit Eagleburg."

Sadly the discoverers of the massacre buried the remains. Then, remounting, they started back for the mountains.

Ten miles south, two figures on horseback slowly rode westward along a beaten trail, rising toward the hills. It was a young man and a young woman, and they were intent on one another.

Fred Carlton was the son of the big Bar C's owner. His father's cattle ranged all this country with other brands, for it was open range. Young Carlton watched the pretty, dark-haired girl on the white mare.

"Elsie, Elsie," he said. "I tell yuh the miners are stealin' our cows. We're missin' hundreds, and I'll bet yore dad will find the same when he checks up."

Carlton was a large young Texan, with tow hair and strong but pleasant blue eyes. He was tanned a rich golden bronze by the Pecos sun and wind. He rode with such ease that he seemed part of his black mustang. Fred had been able to stay on horseback before he could even toddle around the ranch yard. He wore chaps against the chaparral thorns, and a wide

15

brown hat with curved brim. As he smiled at his sweetheart, his teeth showed white and even.

Elsie wore range clothes, too. She was riding like a man and had clean blue overalls on, a short jacket, and a dark hat. Her eyes were appealing, long-lashed and large, her features even and sweet. Her lips, red and full, held Fred Carlton's attention.

"I think you're wrong, Fred," Elsie replied gravely. "The miners from what I've seen of 'em, are hard-working, decent men. They aren't thieves, or killers either."

"Well, that hydraulic minin' sure ruined Sargent Creek," complained Fred. "Water ain't much good when it comes down loaded with mud and muck, Elsie. 'Sides, we can't use them hills for range like we used to."

He looked at the uneven, sparsely grassed ground. There were many bare, almost desertlike spaces. But tough, nutritious grass grew in clumps around the rocks. Though it took a lot of range for the steers, there was plenty of it around. The longhorns would graze over hundreds of miles of such country. But the grass was not what had caught his attention.

"Fresh trail sign!" Fred cried, eyes keening up. "Fifty or sixty cows, Elsie. Driven —

see the shod hoof marks? Say, I've got to find where this leads to! Dad'll want to know, all right!"

CHAPTER II
HATFIELD APPEARS

They rode on in silence. To the south, in a protected valley, stood a wooden line shack, built of stones and with a mud roof. The sign they followed headed directly west toward a gap in the wooded, high mountains.

"A Bar O spread lies through that gap," said Carlton, long face grim. "Now I wonder, Elsie. That syndicate took it over, and I hear it's been made a big spread. Wonder where they got their stock from?"

"Branding mavericks, perhaps."

"Huh! Slow way to build a herd, though there's plenty of wild ones runnin' the hills. Yuh better stay back a way, while I check this."

However, Elsie Wills had pioneer blood in her that coursed as red and strong as in Fred Carlton. She was not the sort to hang back in danger. Up and down, in and out through the tensely wild Pecos land rode the two. They sighted bunches of wild cattle that raised their tails and ran for the bush. The gap wound for miles through the great mountain, wooded on both sides. Sargent Creek came through here, and the formerly clear stream now rolled muddy across its stony bed. The trail followed the north bank of the stream. Where water touched, the growth was lush and green. Tall monitor pines reached their blackly green limbs to the blue sky. The sides were deeply shaded where the sun could not come in.

"I don't like riding through here this way, Fred," Elsie warned.

She was not afraid, though if these were rustlers they had come upon, it would mean trouble.

But the young man was eager to trace the fresh sign. Too eager — for suddenly a bullet whined over his head. The next one, a long slug from a rifle, tore a hole in his high-peaked Stetson.

He jerked hard on his reins and his mustang snapped around.

"Back — Get back, Elsie! We've run on 'em," he shouted. His strong voice echoed through the gap.

The rifle fire, stinging after him, cut up bits of rock and dust at the flying mustang's heels. He winced as a slug bit a chunk from the fleshy part of his left arm. He hurried Elsie's white mare on with a whack of his quirt. They made the turn, out of sight and range of the hidden killer.

"Oh, you're — you're hit!" the young woman gasped, seeing blood welling from Carlton's shirt sleeve. "Let me bind it up —"

"It's nothin' but a scratch. Ride pronto now!"

He was right. Echoing behind came the galloping hoofs of horses. Masked men in corduroy and wide caps, stopped at the eastern end of the gap, hustled them on with bullets that shrieked through the hot air.

The two did not stop until dark, when they drew up at the low, rambling ranch-house of Fred's home, the Bar C. On the wide porch stood a big Texan, raw-boned, with a hooked nose and a hide that looked like sandpaper. He had taken off his Stetson and the bald spot showed, with iron-gray tufts about his ears. His weight was two-forty, but John Carlton, owner and boss of the spread, did not look fat, for he was six-feet-eight in his bare feet. His boots were enormous, his hands like burnt hams. His wintry blue eyes were straight and clear.

"What yuh young rascals mean by runnin'

hosses thataway?" John Carlton boomed, as he saw the lathered steeds.

Fred dismounted. Elsie slid from her saddle as nimbly as a lad, before he could get to her and offer her a hand. They stood there, looking up into the powerful rancher's stern face.

"Dad, we were gunned at Sargent Creek! Got on the trail of rustlers, I'm sure. I told yuh them miners are stealin' our stock. That's how they eat."

Blood burned up under John Carlton's leather cheeks.

"Gunned, and Elsie with yuh? Hey, Sam! C'm out here."

Elsie's father, Sam Wills, who ran the Square 8, southeast of Carlton's spread, came out. In his youth Sam had been lean and dark, but now he had taken on weight. Not so tall as Carlton, he was stout and slower moving than of old. From her father Elsie had inherited her eyes and her strength of will. Sam Wills was a pioneer, an old friend of John Carlton's.

Quickly John Carlton repeated Fred's story. Wills was furious. He banged a hard fist on the porch rail.

"I'm in favor of goin' against them miners!" he snapped.

"Yeah, we'll do jest that. We've stood 'em

roilin' our creek and takin' our hills. But this is too much. I'll git ev'ry rancher in this country to work with us."

"What's yore idea?" asked Sam Wills.

"Those varmints of miners hafta eat. There's a hundred or so up in them hills. Well, we won't let their pack trains go through with any food. We'll drive our cows back so's they can't steal any more. Starve 'em out."

"Sounds like war," Wills growled. "But I'm in favor."

"Yeah, it's war," John Carlton declared. "War to the end. It's them or us."

Capt. William McDowell, veteran Texas Ranger chief, listened with deep attention while the gentleman opposite him made his appeal.

Anson Elms, president of the Pecos Lady Mining Corporation of Austin, Texas, was a thin, elderly man about McDowell's age. He wore thick-lensed pince-nez spectacles and quiet black clothes. Mr. Elms was not a fighting man. He was the sort of decent citizen the Texas Rangers set up to protect, a man of peace and honor, head of an enterprise the state should assist.

"The Pecos Lady mine," Elms was saying, "was opened about a year ago, Captain Mc-

Dowell. We have several hundred stockholders, most of them hard-working good folks who put their savings into our company. David Roberts, our expert, and Ted Morse, who is the manager of the mine, gave us glowing reports as did various assayers. There is no doubt but what there is plenty of gold in the mine.

"Capital was sunk in purchase and transportation of necessary equipment, and more has been used in paying our workers. The first shipment of gold came through safely. It seemed as though we were on the way to fortune, when the trouble began between the ranchers and our employees."

"Yuh say the cowmen object to the hydraulic minin'?" growled McDowell.

"So Roberts reports. In the first raid on our mule train half a dozen men were shot down and the packs stolen. So our Austin board sent George Potter, one of our agents, to the scene. Potter's reports correspond with those of my old friend, David Roberts. There's a taste of actual war now between the cowmen and miners.

"I've come to ask your help, Captain McDowell. Evidently the local law can't handle the situation. It's critical, and in a short time, the Pecos Lady Corporation will go under. You realize what this will mean to our stockholders — complete loss of their whole investment."

The rugged old frontiersman, McDowell, had a grim, strong face. His frame was powerful, but age, showing in his whitened hair, had crippled him so he could no longer ride the trail of Law. But his emotions still flared, hot as they ever had at news of injustice and evil-doers. His face, a rough hide pierced by white whiskers, reddened as he made the inkwell hop with a banging fist.

"Yeah, Elms, I got other reports on what goes on across the Pecos! Sheriff Lew Barnes of Reeves says there's murder and death on the range and it's got beyond him. He claims John Carlton, of the Bar C Ranch, is leader of the cowmen who are raidin' yore gold trains.

"Well, on'y trouble is I knowed John Carlton in Abilene, Kansas, years ago. Carlton was one tough hombre then, and I don't s'pose he's changed any. But he was an honest hombre. Fact, he was chief of vigilantes maintainin' what law there was in them days. Hard to b'lieve he's gone bad. But he's the kind who'll fight for his rights, law or no law. There's on'y one thing for us to do."

"What's that?" asked Elms.

In reply McDowell banged a bell and a scared looking clerk hopped to the door.

24

"Yes, sir, yes, sir," the clerk said hastily.

From the way McDowell had hit the bell he knew the old fellow was enraged by being forced to sit back instead of acting.

"Hatfield still outside?" growled McDowell.

"Yes, sir, yes, sir. I'll fetch him in."

The clerk disappeared like a jack-in-the-box.

Elms watched the open doorway. In a minute it was filled with man. At the sight of him, Elms immediately felt new confidence surging through his discouraged heart.

Well over six feet stood Hatfield, McDowell's star Ranger. Broad at the shoulders so it seemed necessary for him to turn sideward to enter the office, he tapered off to slim hips. From the lean waist of the ace fighting man, hung two blue-steel .45 Colts in black leather holsters well supplied with oil. His slim hands rested quietly at his sides, but they could move with the speed of legerdemain.

Elms' mouth was open in admiration as he took in the superb fighting machine, Jim Hatfield. He saw spurred half-boots, black pants tucked in, the broad leather belt and the cartridge loops full, crossed by a second belt, in which hung the other gun. But it was Hatfield's face which held Elms in fascination. The chin was strong, the jaw was rugged. But the wide mouth was good-humored. This bronzed face, with no fat to it, was dominated by gray-green eyes that could turn cold as a wintry sea. Hatfield was not a pretty man, nor was he even handsome. He was too masculine and strong for that. But he held the observer's eye as a magnet grips steel.

"Want me, Cap'n?" said the Ranger softly.

Elms emitted a deep sigh of breath, re-pressed at sight of the great Ranger. That voice was so gentle, so drawling, that it was deceptive.

"Elms, meet Jim Hatfield," said McDow-ell gruffly. "He'll head for the Pecos. If anybody kin crack that nut, Hatfield kin do it."

Hatfield stood unruffled, long lashes half veiling his eyes, as McDowell quickly told of the terrible trouble reported. He saluted, turned to go.

"Aren't you going to send any men with him?" asked Elms unbelievingly. "Why, there must be hundreds of gunmen involved and the sheriff says it's beyond him —"

A brief smile flitted across Captain Mc-Dowell's seamed face.

"If it's beyond Hatfield," he replied, "then it's beyond all hell-and-gone, Elms. Jest a sec, Jim!"

Hatfield turned in the door, his gray eyes fixing his superior with a steadiness that somewhat reassured Elms.

"Yuh kin ride the river with Lew Barnes, Hatfield. As I told yuh, I knowed John Carlton when he was vigilante chief in Kansas and he was pizen to outlaws then. Carlton caught Cimarron Jones, worst outlaw who ever raided round Abilene, in as brave a piece of law work as yuh'd want to see. Remember, Morse, Roberts and Potter are agents of Elms here. Go to it, then, and straighten out that trouble!"

Elms wiped cold sweat from his brow.

"I hope he makes it," he muttered.

"If he don't," snapped McDowell, "then it can't be made!"

CHAPTER III
HATFIELD
PAYS A DEBT

Out in the brilliant Texas sunlight, Jim Hatfield softly whistled as he saddled up the magnificent golden sorrel. There were men as strong as Jim Hatfield. But, combined with his tremendous strength, went a general's reasoning ability and a speed of coordination never before equaled.

The beautiful sorrel nuzzled his tall master's soothing hand, feigned to nip it.

"So yuh're the wild-and-woolly mustang today," said Hatfield in the level, caressing voice the gelding liked.

He tightened cinches, arranged the Winchester rifle in its leather boot left of the flap, adjusted stirrup straps. Then he swung into the saddle.

Goldy executed a series of bucking movements, while his master sat the leather, apparently part of the horse. Hatfield's wide mouth was amused. When the sorrel had finished his dance, which came from pure exuberance, it lined out and fell into the long, loping stride that ate up the miles.

The Trans-Pecos region had a darkly savage character of its own. On the plateau, the scarcely explored Guadeloupes to the west were the Lone Star state's highest elevation. The wind whipped gritty dust into the tall Ranger's grim face. Streams ran in deep-cut canyons while, above, the earth was dry. Here were tremendous stretches of rocky wilderness seldom looked on by men.

Eagleburg lay in one of the rare oases which even the Trans-Pecos, seeming to relent on occasion allowed to show here and there. The small river, on which the settlement stood, ran through steep banks. But it was not yet too deep in the eroded canyon to be used as a water supply. Herbage was green where the water came in contact with the soil.

Dust layered the rider and golden horse from their incredibly swift ride to the heart of the range war. The sorrel was no longer so sleek. Hatfield's grim face, deep-shadowed by his wide Stetson brim, was drawn with strain. As they came down a steep incline from the east into the valley, the town twinkled with pleasant yellow lamp-lights.

The Ranger's cool gray-green eyes took in

Eagleburg. The main street was lined with crude wooden or stone buildings. Here and there one stood several feet in front of its neighbors, as though trying to steal a start on them. Wooden awnings covered the sidewalks, and there was a plaza in the central part of the little settlement. The main business seemed to consist of saloon-keeping, for there were three of them, and a single musty looking general store.

"Town looks right lively," murmured the tall man.

There were many horses standing outside, reins over the continuous hitch-racks. Music came from the saloons. There were lights on in Keever's General Store. The Ranger noted the long-eared string of mules, with drooped heads and closed eyes, that stood outside it.

Goldy blew alkali from his nostrils, tossed his head. He smelled the water nearby. Hatfield rode to the Eagle Livery Stable, dismounted, and let his pet drink. A young wrangler came forth and greeted him.

"Howdy," said the Ranger. "Lemme take yore comb, sonny." He rubbed Goldy down and wrapped on a blanket. "Give him a grain feed in an hour," he ordered, handing over money. "What's goin' on, sonny?" he asked, as he slapped dust off his clothes. "It ain't Saturday."

"Nope, but a bunch of miners from the Pecos Lady're in town," the wrangler told him. "They're over in the Last Chance Saloon, couple dozen of 'em."

"Them mules belong to 'em?"

"Yeah. And there's a whole passel of cowboys up at the west end. Carlton — he's owner of the Bar C, west of here — is at the Cowboy's Rest with his men."

"Huh? What about it?"

"There's trouble between the miners and cowmen," the wrangler shrugged.

"Ain't there any law here?"

"Well, we got a marshal, but he jest patrols the town. Sheriff's here tonight, though — Lew Barnes."

"And where's he?" Hatfield asked.

"Sheriff's in between, mister. He's down at the Bull's Head saloon. They say he's swearin' in a posse to go hunt the hombres who raided the last gold shipment from the Pecos Lady. Huh, if I was him I wouldn't bother huntin' haystack needles in them Pecos hills. I'd know where to look."

"And where's that?" Hatfield asked shrewdly.

"The Bar C, that's where. The cowmen're raidin' them trains to git even —"

31

The wrangler broke off, biting his lip. He knew he was shooting off his mouth too freely to a stranger. His eyes grew frightened as he took in the tall man's fighting figure, the half-boots and chaps, shirt and vest, wide Stetson with tight chin-strap, and the blue-steel six-guns at the narrow hips.

"Say, yuh're a cowman, ain't yuh, mister? I didn't mean no insult —"

"Forget it, son."

The Ranger tossed him a two-bit piece, started to cross the road toward the Bull's Head. It was his habit to look over a situation before acting. Lew Barnes might have recent information for him, and he meant to contact the sheriff before plunging into the wilds to the great mountains.

Three horsemen, spurring full-tilt along the middle of the road, bore down upon him. They had on leather chaps and jackets to protect them against thorns. Stetsons shaded their faces. Hatfield tried to dodge the charging broncs. The men had evidently been partaking of the bottle. The hombre at the left swerved deliberately, laughing as his horse nearly ran down the tall Ranger.

Hatfield whirled, arm flashing out. He was narrowly missed by the forehoofs of the fast-moving black mustang. But he got hold of the bridle with one hand and let himself drag. His weight jerked the horse around as his boots slid in the dirt. The mustang snorted, trying to rear. But Hatfield held on. The unexpected yank on the reins brought the horseman sideward, so that he nearly fell from his saddle.

Hatfield's quick action had saved him from being bowled over, perhaps badly injured by the bronco's shod hoofs. But it infuriated the half-drunken rider, who cursed violently as he sought to regain his balance.

The man on the black was red-haired, with a pink-fleshed face from which stuck untidy beard ends. He was large, too.

"Hey, Blucher, c'mon," one of his mates called back, looking over his shoulder. For the speed of their mounts had carried them on.

"Leggo that rein, damn yuh," snarled Blucher.

He had a temper to match his red hair. He drew a .45 Colt from his holster, slashed at Hatfield with it.

The Ranger did not speak. He caught Blucher's wrist, breaking the blow, and the gun went off accidentally. The hombre on the black had meant to buffalo Hatfield rather than kill him. The Ranger felt the wind of the nearby slug. Then he stepped back, and Blucher came with him. As the gunny hit dirt, Hatfield twisted the Colt from his hand and slung it away.

"Ugh," grunted Blucher, wind knocked out of him. He lay still for a moment, glaring up at the tall Ranger. Then he set up a howl.

"Hey, Phil, Slim — Help —"

A bullet whirled close to Hatfield, ripping his sleeve. The Ranger squatted down. Slim, the mate of the one who had shot, cried out.

"Look out, Phil! Yuh'll hit Ed!"

Hatfield straightened up. He lifted Ed Blucher with him, and quickly backed to the building line. Then, as Blucher's two pals spurred in at him, he raised one heavy boot, planted it in Blucher's back. With a heave he sent the redhead flying out to crash on his face in the dirt.

The man called Phil fired again. The bullet nicked splinters from the corner of the livery stable. The young wrangler had long since ducked into it and shut the door.

Back in the shadows of the narrow aisle between buildings, Hatfield heard Slim's voice.

"Holster it, yuh fool! Yuh'll warn 'em!"

"Warn who of what?" wondered the Ranger.

Slim evidently had more savvy and sense

than the other two. He caught Blucher's horse and led it to his friend. Blucher was picking himself up and wiping dirt from his scratched, bloody face. People were looking cautiously from windows now. In the Bull's Head doorway stood a tall man, light glinting on a metal badge pinned to his vest flap.

"Here comes the sheriff. Let's duck," Slim growled.

The trio rode frantically through the next opening. In no time they were out of sight. The lawman came over, hunting for the source of the trouble. But there was nobody. The wrangler called from inside the stable.

"Feller tried to run down another one, Sheriff. Nobody hurt."

Hatfield went to the rear of the stable. He looked across a fenced stock corral. Far off he saw the three horsemen pushing furiously toward the west end of town.

To avoid the gathering crowd following the sheriff, Hatfield rounded the back of the livery stable corral and walked west. Carefully he followed the risen dust from the horses of the three with whom he had had his little brush.

"Right salty hombres at that," he mused. "Like to know why Slim was so careful!"

Close to the building-line end, the river

reflecting the yellow lights in streaks on its dark surface, Hatfield saw that the trio had stopped and were dismounting. He kept to the shadows. Stopping a hundred yards away, he watched as Blucher and his two mates took their rifles from the slings. The aromatic breeze blowing toward him brought faint clicks of cocking weapons. Instantly he was ready.

"Got to see what they're aimin' for," he murmured.

He hustled to a point where he could look between dark homes and see the porch of the Cowboys' Rest, which the wrangler had told him was the cowmen's rendezvous.

A couple of cowboys came from the swinging doors. Framed against the lighted windows, they were perfect targets as they paused, rolling cigarets. Hatfield caught the glints off the raised rifles, trained on the saloon.

The Ranger's blue-steel Colt beat the three rifles to it. There was no doubt about what the three gunnies were up to. They plainly meant to pick off the cowboys. Slim squatted a trifle out in front of his mates. His rifle spurted flame a fraction of a second too late. He pitched over on his face. Blucher and Phil wheeled swiftly. Startled by the sudden attack from the shadows behind them, they held their fire.

"Over there by that stable," Hatfield heard Blucher say. "Pick up Slim, quick. We gotta git outa here, Phil."

Blucher began shooting, hunting for Hatfield. But it was a running fire, for they were anxious to get away. Slim's bullet had driven into the porch boards at the feet of his intended victims. The waddies set up a howl, jumped back to call their friends.

Phil slung Slim across his horse. Blucher was out of the Ranger's sight. He heard the sounds of their mustangs' hoofs, but he did not follow out into the light of the street. Cowmen had appeared from the saloon. They were yelling and shooting his way.

Having spiked whatever mischief Ed Blucher and his two pals had been planning, Jim Hatfield hurried back east from the Cowboys' Rest neighborhood.

He waited until the town quieted down somewhat before starting across the dusty road again. Ducking under the continuous hitch-rack, he went up the stoop of the Bull's Head Bar and pushed through the door. Inside were townsmen, some cowboys, a couple of freighters. A tense air hung ominously about the place. As the Ranger shoved in the batwings, men jumped and quickly looked around.

The sheriff came back, grumbling, and disappeared to the rear. He called back over his shoulder to the bartender's question:

"Nothin' at all. Somebody went off half-cocked, that's all."

Hatfield stood at the large bar, while interest in the newcomer subsided. He saw a couple of armed men follow the sheriff through the rear door. When they went in, their vests flapped unadorned. But when they came out shortly afterward, both wore deputy sheriff badges.

Finishing his drink, the Ranger strolled back and walked along a dark hall to a lighted doorway. Inside, the lanky sheriff — a worried hombre of middle age, with drooping brown mustache and a face pleated as a crimson accordion — sat at a wooden table.

"Yuh solemnly swear to do yore duty and uphold law, sohelpyuhGawd —" he was saying with shotgun rapidity, swearing in a chunky cowboy with bow legs.

Sheriff Barnes banged shut the Bible, with an oath of relief, as the cowboy deputy lowered his raised hand.

"There, that's done. Yuh make a baker's dozen, Shorty."

"What, thirteen?" quavered Shorty.

"Git," snapped Barnes. "Be ready to ride

38

at dawn. Furnish yore own hoss and bullets, two bucks a day."

Shorty left. Jim Hatfield went in, softly closing the door into the hall.

"Well?" asked Lew Barnes sharply.

"Evenin', Sheriff," drawled the Ranger.

"Howdy — don't need no more deputies, mister."

"Reckon yuh need *one* more."

"No, dang it, I tell yuh I don't —" began Barnes.

But he stopped short. His narrowed eyes had caught the lamplight shining on the silver star set on silver circle, emblem of the Texas Rangers.

"McDowell sent me," Hatfield told him, taking a chair.

Barnes sat down across the table from him.

"Glad to meet yuh, Ranger. Who are yuh?"

"Hatfield — Jim Hatfield."

CHAPTER IV
RIOT!

Barnes emitted a low whistle. "Huh! I've heard of yuh. How kin I help?"

"Swear me in as a deputy so I can work without ev'ry man-jack in town savvyin' who I am. Second, is anything new?"

"Well, a passel of armed miners pulled into town this afternoon. Claim they was fired on. They're after supplies and blastin' powder. Their bosses, Roberts and Potter, come to kick 'bout losin' their gold shipments."

"How'd they make it this time?" Hatfield asked.

"They had fast hosses and weren't slowed by loads. Gittin' back to the Pecos Lady with their packs may be diff'rent. And — Carlton's brought a bunch of cowboys into town!"

"Wanted to ask yuh 'bout Carlton. Is it his fault?"

Lew Barnes scratched his sandy head,

flecked with gray at the temples.

"Danged if I know, Hatfield. Carlton's one of the bravest hombres I ever knowed. Back in Kansas he busted up the outlaw band of Cimarron Jones. You've heard of that. Cimarron Jones was the worst bandit Kansas ever had — a killer and raider. Hung out in the Territory. He would swoop on the settlements and railroad camps worse than the Injuns. Carlton's famous for catchin' Jones and sendin' him to prison.

"I allus thought Carlton was square as he was brave, till now. The cowmen elected me, but I'm tryin' to play fair and square. There's hotheads on both sides. Both sides've done wrong and yet they got some right, too. Most of them miners're hardworkin', decent fellers. And I've knowed the ranchers many years as good citizens."

A single lamp burned in a wall bracket. The rest were not lit, for no game went on in the sheriff's temporary office, which was donated by the Bull's Head for his use when he was in Eagleburg. His headquarters were at the county seat, many miles northeast. Only urgent necessity brought him to the wilderness.

Looking at the smooth surface of the table between the sheriff and himself, Hatfield turned over the information Barnes gave

41

him. His eyes idly picked out several small particles which lay on the top of the table, without for a time identifying them. When he suddenly realized that the tiny pieces of matter were sawdust, it took all his self-restraint not to look up at the ceiling.

"Well, I'll let yuh swear me in, Sheriff," he drawled. "Then I'll hit the hay. Mighty tired from my ride."

"Okay."

Barnes handed him a deputy badge, which he pinned to his vest flap.

Hatfield opened the door, stepped out into the hall. At the rear end he saw the lower step of a flight leading to the second story. Silently he turned that way. With cat-like tread he passed to the stairs. They were straight and led to the railinged landing of the upper floor.

It was easy to estimate which room was over the one below, where he had sat with Lew Barnes. He glided to it and saw it suddenly drawn to. A bolt inside clicked.

"Cheese it!" a gruff voice inside the thin panel said.

Hatfield leaped. He stood to one side and delivered the door a kick that made the panels crack. In reply a bullet whipped through the wood, tearing a splinter a foot long with it. No light came from the hole.

The room was dark.

Six-gun in hand, he waited an instant. Then he kicked the door again, and it burst in, the bolt ripping from its moorings.

"What's up?" shouted Lew Barnes from below.

Hatfield was too busy to reply. He leaped into the darkened room. A cool draught hit his face. But no more bullets hunted him. Hastily making a search, he found at the side an open window from which the draught was coming. Whoever had been inside the room had taken a quick leave by way of the window. The Ranger stuck out his head and found it was but a short drop to the narrow alley.

He struck a match. The yellow flame lighted the square little chamber. A bunk and chair were the only furnishings to relieve the bare board walls and flooring. From the floor a small metal object caught the light. He stooped, picked up an auger.

Close to his boot was the hole bored through the floor into the room below. The auger had been used to drill through the wooden floor, which formed the ceiling of the cubicle below. He got down on his hands and knees and put his eye to the hole. He could see the table and chairs where

Barnes and he had been sitting a few minutes before.

"Spies," he mused, "watchin' the sheriff."

The bits of sawdust which had dropped from the hole when the auger bit through had warned him. He had figured on something of the sort. Now, he knew, Sheriff Lew Barnes was not the only man in Eagleburg who knew his true connection.

A gunshot smacked in the street. It was like setting off a cap that starts a tremendous chain of explosions. Raucous shouts rang out and six-shooter volleys shook the flimsy windows. Bullets were flying in Eagleburg.

Jim Hatfield jumped to a front window looking out over the wooden awning roof into the road.

Mounted cowboys were riding up and down in front of the Cowboys' Rest, shooting east. Bullets shrieked in the night air. They were giving the Rebel yell, that weird and terrifying cacophony that issues from fighting men's throats in the heat of battle. More and more cowmen were coming from the big saloon. The Ranger glimpsed the huge figure of an hombre who seemed to be the leader. For his long arms were waving and he was evidently giving orders to his men.

Answering rifle and pistol shots came from

the Last Chance to the east. Burly miners from the Pecos Lady hurtled out to take up the gantlet.

In the center of Main Street, like a symbol of the two factions' animosity, a single cowboy, with bowed legs and Stetson strapped on, was having a fist fight with a miner clad in corduroys and knee-high laced boots. They were slugging wildly, throwing all their weight into each blow. Over their heads whirled bullets of hate. The spark had been set to the dangerous powder mine of conflicting ambitions.

Citizens ducked for cover as the riot raged higher and higher. Joined by their pals and led by the big hombre whose stentorian voice could be heard above the din, the mounted cowboys were preparing for a charge. The miners, in a compact bunch, started running to meet them in a life-or-death clash.

"Guess Red Blucher and his pards ain't the on'y ones in on this," muttered Hatfield, as he climbed out onto the awning top.

Double-barreled shotgun gripped in his hands, Lew Barnes came rocketing out of the Bull's Head. He charged right under the Ranger, who squatted on the roof with

45

a ringside seat to the fracas. Several of the sheriff's newly sworn-in deputies followed at his heels.

The sheriff was frantic. He was a good lawman and an honest one. But he had only a couple of minutes in which to stop the two Juggernauts coming together. He let out a roar, shouting at the top of his voice.

As Lew Barnes charged into the road, a stray slug got him and he pitched forward into the dust.

To Jim Hatfield's left, the cowmen under command of the tall man on the dun stallion were forming for the final charge. Outriders were whooping it up, firing their pistols at the miners and riding in wild zigzags in the road. To his right came the miners, slowly, but with a dogged air about them that showed they would not quit.

The sheriff's sudden fall swept away all hope of stopping the riot. His deputies hesitated, loath to step out among those flying bullets —

The Ranger slid to the edge of the wooden roof. He went over, clinging to the front with his hands till he could drop to the plowed-up soft dirt in front of the hitch-rail.

Leaping across Lew Barnes' body, Hatfield had seized the fighting cowboy and miner, who had locked together in a furious embrace. Both men were breathing hard. Swearing, gouging and using their boots, they scrapped, oblivious to all that went on about them.

"Break it up, gents," snapped the Ranger.

The steel of his long fingers dug into the nape of their necks, one hand to each. He choked them off, split them apart. Before they could turn on him, he whipped the cowboy around facing his friends and planted a heavy boot in the man's spine, starting him toward the west end of town. Impartially he used the same foot to kick the miner on his way. The shove gave both a running start.

"Damn! What the hell hit me?"

Hatfield took an instant to squat beside Lew Barnes, who was sitting up, wiping grit from his scratched face. A trickle of blood flowed down the sheriff's pleated red cheek.

"Yuh hurt bad?"

"Naw. Guess that slug musta cut my hair. Jest touched me," muttered Barnes. Suddenly he recalled what was going on, the hard banging of guns bringing back his stunned senses. "I got to stop it —" he gasped, struggling to his feet with Hatfield's help.

"Git down there and check the miners.

I'll talk to the cowmen," Hatfield ordered quickly. "Hustle, now."

Barnes accepted the Ranger's assumption of leadership. There was a power about Jim Hatfield that caused men to obey without question. Shotgun in hand, the sheriff swung east, hurrying toward the miners.

The tall Ranger turned the other way, walking in the center of the road, ignoring the bullets that whistled around him. About seventy mounted men had formed and were coming toward him at an increasingly fast pace. They were cowboys and their bosses, ranchers of the Trans-Pecos. Wild men, veins hot with youthful blood and strength, these were men able to take care of themselves under any circumstances. They carried rifles but preferred the .45 Colt revolver. Under Stetson brims, faces were hardened for the coming fray.

At their head rode a huge Texan with iron-gray hair showing at the sides of his big head. It took a strong horse to carry the weight of such an hombre, though so large was the man's frame that he did not look fat.

Arms swinging easily at his slim hips, Jim Hatfield walked down the middle of the street toward them. He saw the ham-like hands, one holding the reins, the other an old Frontier Model revolver. The boots, shoved into great stirrups, matched the rest of him.

The oncoming cowmen, and the walking Hatfield, came together swiftly. The Ranger stopped ten feet from the huge rancher in the lead and raised a hand high over his head.

"Stop it, mister," he called in a piercing tone of command.

From lamps twinkling on the posts and issuing from the Bull's Head and other windows, the Ranger could make out the strong face under the dark Stetson. He noted the hooked nose with wintry blue eyes at either side of the high bridge, jutting jaw and sandpaper hide. The Ranger knew such men, knew them for what they were — pioneers and individualists who believed in taking care of their own. Clad in cowboy clothing himself, he was safe enough from a deliberately aimed shot, though some of them were still shooting over him at the miners.

"Out of the way," roared the big chief of the cowmen. "Step aside, 'fore I ride yuh down!"

He sought to push the dun past Hatfield. But the tall Ranger stood his ground, feet firmly planted wide apart.

Jim Hatfield's hand leaped out, caught the reins, pulled the dun around. He looked up into the heated eyes of John Carlton.

"Tell yore men to quit shootin', Carlton — Yuh're John Carlton of the Bar C, ain't yuh?"

"Yeah, I am. Leggo that leather, mister. By what right do yuh stop me?"

Hatfield touched the deputy badge on his vest.

"Barnes swore me in tonight, Carlton."

Angry cowboys gathered about the Ranger, who still held to Carlton's reins, preventing the advance.

"Hey, boss. Yuh want us to knock him cold?" demanded a young fellow, gun drawn.

A word from John Carlton and they would beat Hatfield down. But Carlton did not give it. The Ranger's eyes held him, and that fighting power, that fearless nerve at tackling such a bunch single-handed, commanded the rancher's admiration.

That was Hatfield's purpose — to start them talking, arguing. Every minute meant less chance of a bloody, wholesale clash. Down at the east end, Lew Barnes and several deputies had managed to stop the miners. The sheriff was arguing with them and with a couple of men who had come up on horseback who seemed to be the leaders.

"Let him make his talk," ordered Carlton. And he added: "Stop that gun-poppin', dammit, so I kin hear."

Firing ceased altogether. The two groups, only a couple of hundred yards apart, were held in check.

"The sheriff," Hatfield said smoothly, "wishes yuh to take yore men outa town for the night, Carlton."

"Oh he does, huh? This is a free country, ain't it?"

"Shore it's free, but not for riotin'." The Ranger's tone was soft, yet underneath it lay a steel that convinced. "Yuh're makin' a mistake, Carlton, and so're them miners. I tell yuh somebody's eggin' yuh on. I bumped into three of 'em myself, earlier this evenin'. Saw 'em startin' to potshot yuh from the dark."

"Shore, that's what we're fightin' for! The miners begun it. Winged one of my men through a window!"

"The men I seen were not miners."

51

CHAPTER V
DRYGULCHED!

Lew Barnes was hustling to join Hatfield. Coming up, he yelled:

"Listen, John. Git yore boys outa town, will yuh? I'm askin' yuh as an old friend. In the mornin' Potter and Roberts promise they'll start their men west. They're only here for supplies."

"Huh, why should I run away from 'em?" growled Carlton.

"Nobody who knows yuh," said Hatfield diplomatically, "would ever b'lieve yuh'd run from danger, Carlton. The man who busted Cimarron Jones and his gang is no coward."

It was simple truth. Throughout the West, from the Arkansas to the Rio Grande, men of the cow country knew of John Carlton. He was as famous as Wild Bill Hickok and other peace officers of earlier days. The tale was told of how Carlton, his posse shot down, dead or wounded, in the terrible final gunfight with Jones and his bunch, had charged into a mountain hut alone. He shot it out with the surviving Jones and his last two gunnies, had come out with his man. Both of them were wounded, but the law was triumphant. Hatfield knew of Carlton's feat and reputation. Such a man could not be a coward.

"What the sheriff says is sense," the Ranger added.

The huge rancher's face was sour. He scowled but he turned, raised his arm, and ordered his fighting men to swing away.

"Aw right, we'll go," said Carlton. "But I'm not quittin', savvy? There ain't room in this country for them miners and us. They're cow thieves and murderers."

Carlton jerked hard on his reins, pivoted the dun, dug in spurs. Dust rising thick under beating hoofs, the cowboys rode into the darkness westward out of Eagleburg.

"Phew!" sighed Lew Barnes. "Yuh shore kept the undertaker from gettin' rich, Ranger — uh — I mean deputy!"

The two stood, staring after the receding cowmen.

"C'mon," Hatfield ordered. "We'll talk to the miners."

Lew Barnes trotted beside the long-legged Hatfield as the Ranger headed toward the bunched hombres to the east.

Coming to the miners, held in check by Barnes' deputies, the Ranger looked them over quickly. They wore rough clothes and battered felt hats or caps. Many were heavily bearded, living far from civilization as they did. But Hatfield's quick eye decided that they were, for the most, decent fellows. Their hands were toil-hardened to pick and shovel. The eyes that sought the big Ranger's face did not shift. They seemed only to be trying to judge him as he did them.

Besides a couple of big foremen, there were two dressed like engineers, in dark suits and neatly laced boots. They appeared to be chiefs of the miners. One was a large man, with a straight dark hat on curly brown hair, beard stubble curling on his wide chin. The second was older, slimmer and not so tall. He had a shrewd look about him, and grayish straight hair, deep-set black eyes.

"These fellers," explained Lew Barnes, "are George Potter and David Roberts, Jim."

Hatfield nodded.

"Who's this?" demanded Roberts, the smaller of the pair.

"New deputy. We mean to scour the

country for them killers who've hit your gold trains, Roberts."

Roberts flushed, shaking with anger. Potter, too, scowled at the sheriff and his aides.

"You've promised us help and you've never done anything at all, Sheriff," Roberts declared hotly. "A child could tell you it's Carlton and his gunmen who've raided our trains and killed a lot of our men."

"After all," drawled George Potter, "the cowmen elected Barnes."

Lew Barnes gulped, restraining his anger. His face turned a deeper shade of red and his fists were clenched.

"Nobody," he growled, "has ever 'cused me of bein' a crook, Roberts. The cowmen did elect me, but I deal out justice without favor, savvy?"

"Then," Roberts said quickly, "why not catch the murderers and recover the gold from the Pecos Lady?"

"I will," Barnes snapped. "Now disperse yore men, and keep 'em quiet. In the mornin' load up and git goin'."

Potter and Roberts, Hatfield remembered, had been mentioned by Elms in Austin, when the story of the Pecos Lady had been told him. Roberts was a mining expert, and Potter a troubleshooter sent over after the raids began. There was a third, Ted Morse, manager of the mine in the mountains.

Roberts called a sharp order, and the miners turned, went back toward the Last Chance.

"Go to bed, men," Potter called after them. "And keep quiet till mornin'."

The two leaders gave Hatfield and Barnes cold, short nods and followed after their men.

Hatfield and Barnes had stopped the terrible battle that would have meant the death and injury of scores and damage to town property. Now they swung and started up the center of the wide road toward the Bull's Head.

"I need a drink — two of 'em, in fact," Lew Barnes decided.

He swung left, to duck under the hitch-rack and enter the Bull's Head. Deputies trailed Jim Hatfield, who was a short distance behind the sheriff. As the tall Ranger turned his back on the plaza, a rifle spurted fire from a darkened window across the way.

Something irresistible struck the Ranger. He was whipped around. As his hand flashed to his six-gun, drawing and firing a reply by sheer instinct alone, he crashed against the hitch-rack. He rebounded and folded up in the dirt.

The gathering in the dark rear room stopped their talk as a single shot cracked in the night. After the shot, confused shouting began.

"What was that?" growled an hombre, muffled in a black cloak.

"Somebody comin', Chief," rasped another man.

The noise of running footsteps and jingling spurs came from Tin Can Alley, onto which a door of the back room opened. The men in the room drew pistols. The faint metallic clicks told they were cocked.

"Stoppin' here," whispered one.

The steps had paused outside their door. Then somebody knocked.

"Who's that?" a harsh-voiced fellow demanded.

"It's me, boys — Al!"

The man nearest the door opened it, letting in a dim shaft of light. Outside stood a thin, dark-haired man in cowboy garb. He had sneering, thin lips curved at one side, a sharp pointed nose and close-set dark eyes. The big man who had pulled back the door showed. He wore a bandage over his red hair, a rough cloth tied on, through which the dark stain of blood seeped.

"Hullo, Blucher," the thin devil said, stepping inside.

Blucher, the red-haired man whom Jim Hatfield had bested earlier in the night, shut the door with a curse.

"Well, Osman, what's up?" the man in the cloak demanded from the shadows.

Al Osman was breathing hard from running.

"Looka, Chief," he said quickly. "I jest shot a Ranger!"

"A Ranger!" repeated the Chief. "A Texas Ranger?"

"Yeah. Yuh see that big jigger, who stopped the fight yuh got up tonight?"

"Yeah. One of Barnes' new deputies."

"Damn his heart and soul," swore Ed Blucher. "That skunk near finished me, Chief. It'll be a month 'fore pore Slim kin fork a bronc agin."

"Well, he's a Ranger spy!"

The Chief cursed hotly. "How do you know that?"

"Mike and me were watchin' Barnes swear in his posse — so's we'd savvy who his men are and what he's up to, as yuh ordered. Barnes took on a dozen, then quit. In strolls this big jigger and interduces hisself as Jim Hatfield, from Austin. Asked a bunch of questions. He's here to stop the Pecos Lady trouble, says he. I seen his Ranger star when he showed it to Barnes.

"He's smart, too — or was, anyways. He caught on someone was listenin' upstairs and tried to rush us. We on'y got out the winder with a minute to spare. I lay low and when I got the drop on him, I let him have it."

"Hope yuh kilt him," snarled Blucher.

"Figger I did," boasted Osman. "Aimed for his head, Chief, and he went down like he was axed. He fired a shot that hit the wall, but I reckon it was instinct. I run out back, circled around, and come here. They're huntin' the other side of the plaza now."

"Huh," grunted the Chief. He was turning this new development over in his cleverly fiendish mind. "I don't like this, boys. If that Ranger saw Ed, Slim and Phil pot-shottin' at Carlton's men he might guess. Well, mebbe he ain't reported to Austin on that yet. Kansas Phil, go circulate around and find if that Ranger's really done for. If he is, we have another two or three weeks to work, with on'y the sheriff to buck."

Kansas Phil, one of the trio whom Hatfield had bested before the Ranger was drygulched by Al Osman, slipped out into Tin Can Alley and the door was bolted after him. The sinister gathering awaited his return. As they inhaled, ruby glows of brown-paper cigarets lighted up their brutal faces.

Inside of twenty minutes Kansas Phil came back, giving the signal which opened the door.

"He's dead!" he cried. "They carried him into the Bull's Head. Barnes jest come out from the back room and said he's done for."

Sighs of relief were audible. None of these hombres fancied bucking the Texas Rangers if it could be avoided. But the Chief was none too satisfied.

"Osman," he said, "here's a fifty-dollar bonus for pluggin' that Hatfield snake. He was McDowell's star ranger, though. McDowell's probably goin' to pull ev'ry Ranger he can lay his hands on and rush 'em here. It'll mean a troop snoopin' around and botherin' us. And there's the chance Hatfield told Barnes he suspicioned there were other parties in this besides miners and cowmen. We've got to figure how to block the Rangers and the sheriff. Make dead certain we stay hidden."

They were silent, waiting for their leader's

decision. Finally Al Osman growled.

"Well, I don't like Texas Rangers, Chief. Buckin' 'em's diff'rent from ordinary law. What about Carlton?"

Mention of Carlton's name caused the Chief to curse with such insane fury that even the killers with him felt their hackles rise in shivery dread. It was a bestial hate, the insane lust of a wild beast.

"Carlton's got to pay," declared the Chief. "And I've figured how to do it right and fool the Rangers and Barnes at the same time. The attacks on the miners got to be laid on the cowmen dead to right. That'll cover us and give us freedom to move as we like. Once Barnes and McDowell're convinced it's altogether the ranchers, they'll lay off huntin' further. Then we won't have Rangers and posses snoopin' over the country. Here's how we'll work it, boys."

He drew on his brown-paper cigaret. The glow reflected red fire from his half-closed eyes, as he gave precise directions and orders to his cronies.

Al Osman sighed with admiration when the Chief had finished.

"Yuh're damn smart, Chief," he declared. "It'll work perfect. Now, I reckon we better ride, if we're to git ahead of them miners. We'll hit 'em Thursday. They'll travel slow with them loads goin' back to the mountains."

The chief rose, dark figure bulking against the pale rectangle of the window.

"*Hasta luego,* gents," he growled, and slipped from the room, hurrying down the alley.

The others hitched up their gunbelts. Horses were fetched from the broken-down stable across the way. The wounded Slim was loaded on the back of a horse. He swore as they jolted his wound. Red Ed Blucher could ride, and he kept chuckling as he thought of the dead Ranger whose fault it was that he was injured. It kept him cheerful.

"I'd've kilt him myself but yuh saved me the job, Osman," he remarked.

The mounted gunmen kept out of lighted areas. Well north of Eagleburg, they hit the bush and swung west in the darkness.

CHAPTER VI
ARREST

The redness of the dawn woke Fred Carlton, in his bunk at the Bar C ranch house. He was quickly up, already dressed in his riding clothes, save for the heavy leather chaps and silver spurs. Those he would add later when he went to saddle up.

The Chinese cook had breakfast ready for him. He ate in the kitchen, a hearty meal showing that nothing could spoil a young man's appetite. The clear air of the Trans-Pecos, and the hard manual labor that was called for, kept a fellow from being finnicky about his food.

Finishing his third cup of coffee, and polishing the various plates of beef and bread, he rose and strolled through into the big living room.

"Dad oughta be home soon," he murmured aloud.

His father had ridden to Eagleburg, leaving his son in charge of the spread. A rider had come over from Ulman's Flying U, twenty miles east. He'd brought word that John Carlton and his friends had just come in from town, but that it might be two or three days before Fred could expect his dad home. In charge of operations against the Pecos Lady miners, whom the cowmen had followed to Eagleburg, John would have his hands full.

Though not the giant his father was, Fred Carlton was a six-footer, hitting the scale around two hundred pounds. His tow hair and blue eyes were a very common coloring in Texas. But Fred was unusually pleasant in disposition until he was riled. Then some of his father's fiery nature would flare up in him.

For a moment the young man stood before the two crossed six-shooters hanging from a wooden peg in the wall. They were old-style cap-and-ball Colts, the walnut stocks filigreed with heavy, hand-beaten gold. A brace of beautifully made, expensive pistols, in their time they had been the very best that money could buy. There had been rapid improvements in guns in the past eleven years, but these were still good.

From his boyhood, Fred had stared at these wonderful guns. He had stood there as before a shrine. He knew the great story of them. They had belonged to Cimarron Jones, the brutal bandit chieftain who had terrorized Kansas and the Nations. They spelled what his father was — bravest of the brave, a leader of men — for it was John Carlton who had finished the outlaw's terrible career of blood, and taken away the guns of Cimarron Jones.

Five years ago Fred's mother had died. In trouble, the youth had found comfort and new strength in his father's prowess. And John Carlton, taking Fate's blows with the fortitude he had displayed in all of life, loved his only son with a fierceness hidden under the Texan's taciturnity and dislike of displayed emotion.

John was mighty proud of Fred, of the younger Carlton's riding ability and skill on the range, of his decency and fine character. In protecting the empire he had carved from the cruel Trans-Pecos, John Carlton was also protecting his son's future.

Hard as this life was, Fred had grown up to it. He loved it. The price of cattle was rising, and it seemed that these cattlemen might look forward to a more full existence — Or so it had appeared until the Pecos Lady trouble came upon them.

Fred saddled up, donned chaps and spurs,

strapped on his Stetson. With a wave of his arm to the cook, who was hanging out wash in the back yard, he rode west under a warming sun. He meant to ride close to the ranch and inspect what cattle had been driven over from the west hills, out of reach of the thieving miners of the Pecos Lady. For the Carltons were convinced that they were stealing cows from the range for food.

He crossed Sargent Creek on a bridge made of strong logs. The canyon here was deepening but the Bar C raised water by means of windmills. The pumping kept the stream muddy. But a feeder brook came from the south. Falling into the creek, it gave them enough fresh water for drinking and cooking. The stock used the muddied liquid from the tanks.

Bunches of cattle, Bar C and other brands ran the common range. Whistling with sheer joy of living, the husky young rider spurred his black-and-white mustang west.

The range dipped up and down in long, sandy slopes. Rocks and tough grasses rose to the mountains, blue against the golden sky. Fred was out of sight of the house, down behind one of these dips. From a thick mesquite clump, a quarter mile ahead, he saw a man spurt out and quirt his chestnut mustang full-tilt in the opposite direction.

For a moment Fred thought it was one of his own punchers. But he didn't recognize the rider or the horse. The startled flight was so puzzling that he increased his pace and followed.

Cautiously pushing through a narrow gap between buttes, he came out onto a plain dotted with stones and sagebrush. The stranger had slowed down and was looking back over his shoulder. When he caught sight of Fred, he again began running away.

"Now what the devil's he up to?"

Sore at the rustling and pot-shotting that had been going on, Fred felt a rush of excitement as he took up the chase.

At the summit of the next wavelike rise in the plain floor, the wind brought to him the familiar odor of burnt hide and hair. It was the smell that comes only from a branding-iron laid on the flank of a steer or horse.

"So that's it," Fred growled. "He was look-out."

He was cautious now, for if there were any number of the thieves, he would need help. His men must be working to the north, and he might call them. . . .

But reaching the following ridge, he could look over and see what went on. The man he was chasing had come up to a second hombre, given him warning. The latter had left the hogtied yearling lying where it had fallen when roped. Now he was leaping into his saddle. Half a dozen picked two-year-olds stood close by. Right under Carlton's nose, the pair of cow-thieves brazenly began driving them west, yelling and quirting the beeves on.

"What a nerve!" Fred exclaimed. "I'll make 'em drop them dogies quick enough!"

He touched his black-and-white with a spur. They were hitting full-speed for the foothills and mountains, running before them the long-horns, who could go about as fast as a horse when they wished.

In the heat of the chase, Fred stuck on them. The rising dust was so cloggingly thick that he raised his bandanna, to sift some of it from the air he breathed. He meant to stick on these rustlers and see exactly where they went. At least he would prevent them from taking the small bunch they had.

Aware that there might be more of them around, he kept a sharp eye open. But he did not see any others. Drawing his Colt .45, Fred fired a couple of shots after them. They were too far off for six-gun range. He figured his friends would hear the explosions and follow him up.

Mile after mile rolled behind him. Tantalizingly the pair of thieves before him kept just out of reach. The going was harder now, the land cut up by buttes and razor-topped ridges. He had to make sure he was not being ambushed. But each time he worked to where he could see ahead, the two hombres with the Bar C steers were still driving a good distance before him.

Across Sargent Creek, which ran between fordable banks here, stood a small line shack in a deep little valley. To Carlton's surprise, the rustlers, instead of continuing on toward the mountains, swung the steers that way.

"I'll git 'em now," he growled, following them up.

The shack, built into the hillside, came into his full vision. The door stood open. The rustlers ran the cows past it and Carlton followed into the cut.

Suddenly he yanked his black-and-white to a sliding stop. Several more riders had come from the bush and rocks south to join the thieves. Fred turned to retreat. More men now blocked his way out. A cold sweat broke on him as he realized he had walked straight into a trap.

The sun glinted on the guns and polished gear of the men slowly closing in on him.

They were masked to the eyes. Fred knew this terrain by heart. There was but one thing to do — hole up in the line shack and hold them off till help came.

"Reckon the boys'll be along some time," he muttered.

He threw himself from his horse, slapping the animal. He had left the reins up so the mustang would run out of danger. No use to let them take or shoot down his horse.

A bullet shrieked past the door, a foot behind Fred. He jumped inside the shack. Drawing his Colt, he stepped to the side of the tiny hole which served as a lookout window on the north. There was an old iron stove in one corner, a couple of rough bunks, and two boxes standing on the dirt floor.

Carlton stuck his six-gun out the hole and fired a shot that kicked up dust between the horsemen to the north. They stopped, sent some bullets that whirled high. They did not even strike the shack.

"Mighty pore aimin'," grunted Fred. "Funny."

The whole affair was strange, but he didn't suspect the motive. The men south were drawn back out of sight. Those from the north, evidently not liking his bullets, also faded out of the valley. Silence fell upon the range.

"Wonder if they're tryin' to draw me out?" he muttered.

Fred stepped to the door. It was fairly dark inside the single-windowed hut when the door was shut. He opened it a foot, stuck his Stetson out on the end of his long-barreled pistol. A bullet shrieked by. He drew back and sat down on one of the boxes, ears wide, listening in case they tried a rush.

"Suits me to wait," he thought. "The boys'll shore be along after awhile."

For an hour Fred waited; alert. Nothing happened. He was beginning to get bored. Constantly peeking out, he had seen no signs of the enemy at either end.

Then to his keen ears came the sound of hoofs pounding from the north. Gun gripped in hand, he jumped to the window and saw men in cowboy clothing pushing their horses toward the shack. They weren't his riders. He could tell that. He fired a hasty shot over their heads that brought a reply in the form of a businesslike volley. It tore into the logs of the shack within inches of the little loophole.

Fred ducked, bobbed up to shoot again, only to gasp and hold his fire. A lanky hombre had spurted into the lead. He had his bandanna drawn up, but that might be only to guard against the biting dust of the region. The sun gleamed on the sheriff's star pinned to his flapping vest.

"Sheriff Barnes!" exclaimed Carlton, and ran over to open the door.

As he emerged, Barnes fired a shot at him that cut a hole in Fred's leather chaps. He stepped back, crying out in amazement.

"Throw out yore guns, Carlton!" Barnes shouted.

"Aw right, Sheriff," Fred replied, tossing out his gun-belt. "Dunno what's goin' on, but either me or you is loco!"

Barnes approached. With him were a dozen men from Eagleburg — his posse. He kept his eyes on Fred all the while.

"I didn't reckernize yuh at first look, Sheriff," Carlton told him. "I'd never've sent that shot over yuh."

"Huh," grunted Barnes. "Watch him, boys. Sorry to see yuh here, Fred." He had known young Carlton for many years.

Barnes' seamed face was beet-red as usual. His washed-out eyes had a sad but grim expression. He went into the line shack while deputies gathered silently about Fred Carlton, and began rolling cigarets.

"What's this all about?" Fred asked,

deeply puzzled. "I chased some rustlers here. They made me hole up in the shack. After a while they faded off along yuh come —"

"Yeah?" growled Shorty Olliphant. "Shore sorry to see yuh here, Fred," he added, his voice low and sad.

They all seemed sorry about it. Puzzled, Carlton looked around over his shoulder. Lew Barnes was digging behind the rusted cookstove. Presently the sheriff called.

"C'mere, Shorty. I got it."

Curious deputies pressed inside, shoving Fred ahead of them. The open door gave light. The sheriff stooped, lifting several objects covered with bagging from the shallow hole he had scooped.

"Gold!" gasped Fred.

Chapter VII
Return from
the Dead

Pulled aside, the bagging disclosed unmistakable blocks of gold. Barnes pointed to one of the stamps.

"Pecos Lady," he growled. "This is from one of them murder raids, gents."

Fred still didn't savvy the full import of this. He shoved back his Stetson, scratched his tow-haired head.

"Danged if that ain't queer, that bein' in our line shack. Reckon there's any more, Sheriff?"

Barnes gave him that look again, half anger, half sorrow.

"Mebbe I oughta ask you that, Fred," he replied quietly.

Possemen were digging all around the hut, but no more caches were uncovered.

"Where's the rest of it, Fred?" the sheriff inquired. "Tell me and save me the trouble, boy. Yore dad in on this, too? Or was it you young hot-heads done it all?"

"Yuh're crazy," snapped Fred. He had finally realized that they thought he was guilty; had buried the gold. "I didn't savvy it was there."

"This is shore enough proof, Sheriff," Shorty Olliphant said gravely. "That 'nonymous tip hit the nail on the head."

"Somebody sent yuh here, Barnes?" asked Carlton.

The officer nodded. From his shirt pocket he took out a small piece of white paper. Puzzled lines deep in his brow, Fred looked over his shoulder and read:

Sheriff, if yuh reelly want to catch the killers ask Fred Carlton. Behind stov in Bar C line shack.

The writing was a scrawl, there was no signature.

Lew Barnes rapped out orders. The gold bars were fastened in saddlebags. He pulled a pair of large, old-fashioned handcuffs.

"Fetch his hoss, Jake," he called.

The black-and-white was lassoed and brought up. Fred mounted, then Barnes cuffed his hands to the saddle-horn.

"We'll bear north, boys," the sheriff ordered. "No doubt but the Bar C waddies'll try to snatch him from us if we run into

75

'em. We better keep outa their way. I don't want no unnecessary fuss."

Fred Carlton shrugged. He still couldn't believe they thought him guilty of those cold-blooded massacres and the theft of the Pecos Lady gold. Lew Barnes was a square shooter. Fred was sure of that. The lean officer would see justice done to the best of his ability.

The little cavalcade rode out of the valley. Fred Carlton was surrounded on all sides by grim-faced, armed deputies. Shorty Olliphant, who had very keen eyesight, took the lead, scouting the way and watching for any signs of approaching riders.

"Where yuh reckon on takin' me to, Lew?" asked Fred.

He was upset inside, but he held himself well. His shoulders were squared, his handsome face apparently untroubled.

"Takin' yuh to Eagleburg jail, Fred," answered the sheriff.

The muscles of the big horses rippled as the beasts made their way along the uneven trail, skirting boulders and thorned plants. Crossing Sargent Creek, they started in a northeast direction. But they angled off so they might circle the immediate neighborhood of the big Bar C, where Fred Carlton's cowboys were concentrated. The sun touched the mountain tops, bathing them in a bloody hue, symbolic of the death that gripped the range.

Shorty Olliphant came trotting back, reined up in front of Lew Barnes.

"Some dust up ahead, off to the west, Sheriff," he reported. "Can't see nobody yet, but it's a rider, I'm shore."

"Huh," grunted Barnes. "Hope it ain't Carlton's pals."

He was worried about holding on to his important prisoner. If attacked, he would have to use force, although he hated the thought of entering a gunfight against cowmen. They were his own kind, many of them old friends who had backed him. Yet he was fair and square, determined to see the Law take its course in this matter.

There was a dense clump of mesquite covering a sharp-topped ridge to the right. The bottom of the draw was lined with boulders which showed, from their rounded contours, that water had at some time flowed here.

"Take him in there, boys," ordered Barnes quickly. "I'll sashay up and see who it is. Mebbe I kin turn 'em. Lie low, now, till I come back or yuh hear shootin'."

The sheriff nodded, jerked his reins. He

pushed his rangy horse into the rising foot-hills, where scrubby pines broke the skyline.

Jim Hatfield had spied the sheriff's posse several minutes before Shorty Olliphant's keen eyes had picked up the Ranger's dust trail in the sky. He had been coming south, keeping to shale and matted grass, so there might be no rising dust behind him. Not till he had been able to identify the posse as friends had he turned and taken the easier course. Then Shorty had observed the approaching dust cloud in the air.

The tall Ranger's face showed deep lines of pain and stress. His Stetson was strapped back, off the wadded bandage on the deep scalp wound he had taken from the drygulcher in Eagleburg. His black hair had been roughly cut short around the jagged lips of the wound. Fresh bleeding, brought on by the motion of the horse under him, had clotted there, sticking bunches of hair to the flesh behind his ear.

Blackness had overcome Jim Hatfield when that bullet struck. It had been a reflex action, keened by the superb natural powers of the Ranger, which had made it possible for Hatfield to draw and fire before he hit the dust. Even though he was dangerously clipped, Jim Hatfield had ducked his head under the hitch-rail outside the Bull's Head. Only that fact had saved him from instantaneous death. A half-inch lower and it would have meant a smashed brainpan.

He had recovered his senses after Lew Barnes and Shorty Olliphant had toted him into the back room at the Bull's Head. Barnes had shooed away the crowd, shut the door, kept him quiet until the sawbones could be fetched. Finding where he was, the Ranger had feigned to be worse hit than he was. Eyes veiled by long lashes, he had watched for his opportunity. Barnes was alone in the room with him. A couple of deputies were posted outside the door.

Hatfield wanted a chance to work under cover until he had surveyed the situation in full. He had seen just the necessary event which would throw his hidden enemies off guard for a time, till he could get his investigation rolling. A whisper to Lew Barnes, who cursed his relief at finding the Ranger only creased, and the trick was effected.

The old doctor was a pal of Barnes. He dressed the wound while Barnes kept the door locked. When he went out, sadly shaking his head, he announced Hatfield's death. Covered with a blanket, the "body" had been carried out on a board by Barnes and Shorty, dumped into a wagon the sheriff borrowed. Lew Barnes drove away, ostensibly to bury the remains.

The sheriff had brought up Goldy secretly. Hatfield had hit the bush, ridden north, and then swung west. There he started his hunt in the wilderness. He had had a look at the death gap where the pack-trains had been attacked. He was hunting a hole through to the other side of the mountains when he sighted the sheriff's posse.

Seeing Lew Barnes coming out ahead, he observed the deputies quickly plunging into the mesquite with a man who was apparently a prisoner. Hatfield waited, screened by a clump of pines. He was in no hurry to give up the advantage of having people consider him dead. However, Lew Barnes had connived with him in this. Now he desired a word with the sheriff, if only to inquire the best way through the hills. They had agreed they might connect to the west when Barnes came over with his men.

Lew Barnes was on the alert. Hatfield could tell that by his narrowed eyes, the tenseness of his body as he sat his leather. The way Barnes carried his right arm, hand swinging close to holstered six-gun, was a pure betrayal.

"Wonder what he's run onto," mused Hatfield.

He let Barnes spot him then, by pushing the sorrel out a bit. Barnes' face relaxed in relief as he spurred over to the tall Ranger's side. He swung his horse for a parley, pulling down his bandanna so he could talk.

"Howdy, Hatfield," Lew Barnes greeted him. "Glad to see yuh."

"That a pris'ner yuh got?" Hatfield inquired.

"Yep. It's all settled, Ranger. I got a 'nonymous note tellin' me to watch for Fred Carlton in a line shack, south of here, across the creek. Shore enough, I caught Fred redhanded. He fired a shot at us. But, seein' he was outnumbered and his hoss havin' wandered off a ways, he give up. Tried to lie outa it but I dug up somethin'. Look."

From a bulky saddle-bag, Barnes extracted one of the bars he had found cached under the stove in the line shack.

Hatfield looked it over curiously. He saw the crudely stamped Pecos Lady stamp.

"That's shore enough gold," he agreed. "And it's from the mine, too. Fred is John Carlton's only son, ain't he? Does he admit anything, now yuh've caught him?"

"Nope, nacherly not. I ain't s'prised the cowmen done it, Hatfield. On'y the low

81

meanness of them massacres hits me awful hard. I feared the ranchers was hittin' the miners, to skeer 'em out. This cinches it. No use lookin' further."

It wasn't, the Ranger thought. Just as the sheriff said, it was amazing that the cowmen were behind all the slaughter and robbery. Still, the methods used did not fit in with the nature of strong men, such as John Carlton.

"Jest what does Fred Carlton say about yore ketchin' him in that shack with the gold?" Hatfield drawled.

"He's sore, and now he's worried. Says he was led there by a coupla rustlers. Then he was held in the shack by a bunch of masked gunmen. Claims he had nuthin' to do with the gold, didn't know 't was there."

"And how'd he wriggle outa the pot-shot he took at yuh?"

"Didn't reckernize us. He was too excited and thought it was his enemies comin' back. It's shore a lame talk he gives."

"Well — If it was Fred Carlton and his pals," Hatfield mused aloud, "that shore 'll make this war tough!"

Lew Barnes shrugged. "No doubt of it, Ranger. Yuh comin' back to town now? Ain't much use in yore stayin' hid since it's proved it's the ranchers raidin' the gold trains. Fred 'll furnish the key to the whole dirty game. And I mean to work on him."

"Reckon I'll jest check up a little more," drawled Hatfield. "There's still a few things don't altogether jibe, Sheriff."

"Okay," shrugged Lew Barnes. "Suit yourself. Anything I kin do for yuh, lemme know."

"One thing I'd like, and that's a peek at Fred Carlton. But I want to stay under cover," Hatfield said. "S'pose I come down a ways. You swing past that big grove of junipers. Keep yore men movin', but make shore Fred's where I kin have a look at him."

"Okay, I'll do that. *Adios,* then, Ranger."

"*Adios,* Sheriff."

Hatfield left the sorrel back in the pines. On foot he strolled to the junipers. Lew Barnes rode over to the draw where his posse lurked. He signaled Shorty, and the cavalcade emerged. Barnes gave them some explanation about the rider whose dust they had glimpsed. The story satisfied them, and they came swinging up past the spot where the Ranger was concealed. Having paid for his advantage with the head wound that had come so close to killing him, Jim Hatfield wanted to get a good start before he again showed himself in the open.

Barnes rode at the rear. He had cut out Fred Carlton and placed him on the side next the juniper clump. He made an excuse to stop, feigning it was to light up a quirly he had rolled. He bumped his horse against Carlton's black-and-white, turning Fred toward Hatfield.

Hatfield scrutinized the young prisoner. Fred's face was smudged with dirt, his clothing ripped and sweated. But Jim Hatfield could pierce behind that.

"Huh," he grunted. "He don't look like the kind who hides behind bushes and shoots innocent men in the back! It ain't in his blood, either."

In fact, he liked the way Fred Carlton held himself. He could see the clear gleam of the young fellow's eyes and the square set of his big shoulders.

Barnes swung on. As they dropped behind a rise to the northeast, Hatfield returned to his horse. He mounted and rode on south. He crossed the creek and headed for the line shack.

"I still wanta know what them three was up to, drygulchin' the Cowboys' Rest that night," he muttered aloud to his horse. "And Fred Carlton don't have a killer's look at all. Mebbe his story's true, at that."

Those spies watching the sheriff, the other

unexplained clues he had run upon, called for an answer. Jim Hatfield would not stop until he was satisfied.

Down in the narrow valley, where the line shack stood, the tall Ranger dismounted and looked over the tracks he found.

The underfooting was dry and the posse had cut up the ground around the shack. But a mile south he came upon fresh tracks. To his right, a bit of scored mica in a rock-ledge caught his alert eye. He swung to it, for the scintillating stuff was a clear sign that someone had recently been here.

It was hard going, but up above he found unmistakable evidence that men had come through the bush within a few hours. He trailed on, reached the top after a hard climb. Keeping on the trail, he came back on Sargent Creek and crossed to the road leading through the pine-shaded gap.

"So far, so good," he told Goldy. "Carlton spoke the truth 'bout that. These fellers, whoever they are, put him in that shack for the sheriff!"

The sorrel shivered his golden hide. They rode slowly westward in the winding gap, the creek rolling muddy to the south. The trail turns were hairpin. The tall Ranger's eyes were always ahead, in the blue shadows, for he did not fancy this road. Not because of peril, but because it was the sort of pass that could easily be watched — and would be, by guilty men —

Goldy sniffed, snorted a warning. His keen animal senses had caught something that spelled danger. The Ranger jerked his rein. The sorrel swung close against the tall red cliff to the right. At the same instant a bullet shrieked through the air, rapped into the rocks down the bend.

"Huh! We ain't welcome," he muttered, drawing a Colt and peering up ahead at the heavily wooded slopes.

There was no way up at the place. It was obvious suicide to ride the constricted pass in daylight. There were sentries up in the woods, lying behind barricades of tree trunks or stones. All they were waiting for was to have him try to climb. . . .

Chapter VIII
The Pecos Lady

Jim Hatfield dismounted. He placed his Stetson on the end of his six-shooter, poked it out a bit around the edge of the cliff. Immediately two rifle bullets, fired at almost the same instant, tore from the woods. One nipped his felt.

"Good shootin', Goldy," he grudged. "Got to go around the other way, I reckon."

Mounting, he turned and rode back to the eastern mouth of the deep gap. From the direction of the Bar C, he heard far-off whoops. His keen eyes made out the approaching band of cowboys, a dozen or so of them. They had seen him come out of the gap. As they swept on toward him, they began shooting at him.

"Hostile, too," remarked the Ranger.

His quick eye took in the terrain. The high wooded shoulders of the mountain formed the main gap through which Sargent Creek made its way past the hills to the lower lands. The south seemed better. Northward lay the Pecos Lady mine, which he meant to inspect at the earliest possible moment. Now he had to think about getting away from the cowboys who were riding westward.

The sorrel picked up speed. It cut to Sargent Creek, sliding down the steep clay bank. After the wade, it struggled up the south side. He galloped, twisting in and out of broken chaparral. The cowboys came to the spot where he had crossed, sent bullets his way. But they did not follow. Instead, they turned and rode west.

"Wonder what'll happen when they hit that trap," he said aloud.

Half an hour later, as he worked up the side of the mountain shoulder, he heard faint volleys from the gap.

The slope grew so steep that he could no longer stay in the saddle. It was too much for a horse carrying a burden. He dismounted and led the sorrel, whose hoofs slid as he dug them in.

Close to dark he reached the summit of the mountain shoulders. Sweat and dirt covered man and horse as the Ranger gazed out over the terrible wilderness of the Trans-Pecos. East ran Sargent Creek through its deepening canyon. South rose sharp-tipped mountains — jagged country fit only for the rattlers and wild beasts that inhabited it. West stretched the gap trail, out of his sight under the steep sides of the precipices, too close in for him to command. But farther west he saw smoke.

"Reckon that'll be the A Bar O Ranch they mentioned," he muttered.

The firing he had heard had long since stopped. But his keen eyes sighted the cowboys, drawn off to one side east of the gap entrance. They had dismounted. Now they squatted in a circle, evidently waiting.

In gathering shadows, the blood-red sun tipping the far-off mountains of the next range, the Ranger started to work down the west slope. It was much easier going. Stars came twinkling into sight as the sun dropped and a slice of pale moon came up. He came to comparatively level ground.

Mounting, he rode north until he was quite close to the twinkling lights of a big ranch. It was set at the elbow bend made by Sargent Creek as it swung down out of the north and turned through the gap, changing from mountain torrent to creek. The sound of its stepped falls down the beaten rocks dominated the neighborhood. It drowned out the clop of Goldy's hoofs, the noises of the bush.

The road leading from the gap crossed the high-banked creek on a bridge of logs. Behind the ranch house were corrals and outbuildings, flat spaces in the natural valley. To the north the slopes rose, dark and wooded.

He had no doubt the bridge, too, was carefully guarded. But they would not expect trouble from the west. He rode within a couple of hundred yards of the outermost corrals. Then he left Goldy hidden behind some mesquite that jutted black from the flats.

Hatfield had hardly started his secret survey of the A Bar O when the sound of hoofs drummed upon the earth. The sound sent him down low, crouching in the shadows. A large band of men rode out of the woods of the northern slopes. They pounded up to the house and dismounted.

There were fifty or sixty of the riders. From what Hatfield could make out, they wore cowboy clothes and were heavily armed. For a time there was the confusion of men hanging up saddles, stretching their limbs after a long ride, cursing as a stubborn buckle refused to open.

"Okay, Mike," a gruff-voiced, slender

hombre called. "Run 'em up into the woods."

Three or four of them began to drive off the band of horses, lathered and mud-covered, which had been ridden in. The majority of the men went inside the big house, calling for food.

"Quite a spread, and night work at that," murmured Hatfield, stalking closer. "Now, why push their ponies into the woods?"

In the corrals he had passed, he had seen plenty more mustangs.

They evidently felt safe behind their guarded trails. He came up close to a window and looked through. The hombres who lounged around, drinking and eating, wore cowmen's duds. But they had hard, bearded faces and their weapons were evidently much used.

Sitting in front of the fireplace was a tall, thin devil with a sharp nose and twisted lips. He had taken off his Stetson. The thin, sweat-matted black hair stuck to his olive-skinned forehead. He was busy cleaning a fine Winchester rifle, which he seemed much taken with, for it was a pet weapon that he carefully attended.

The Ranger's eyes traveled about the big room, filled with gunmen. From information given him he understood the A Bar O had been taken over after the death of its pioneer owner by a syndicate. The spread was now run by a man named Al Osman. Hatfield stopped his inspection. He gazed at the fellow slouched on a bunk near Osman.

"Dawgone if it ain't my wounded friend Slim!" Hunting on, he saw the redhead with whom he had had the brush in Eagleburg that night. "And there's Red Blucher, too — and Phil! Why, it's like old-home week."

A shrill war-whoop knifed from the gap trail. It startled not only the Ranger but the entire gathering of gunnies.

"What the hell's that, Osman?" cried Red Ed Blucher, snatching up a pistol.

Hoofs thudded on the log bridge across the creek. A couple of men whirled up, threw themselves from their lathered horses.

"What's wrong, Barney?" demanded the thin hombre, Al Osman, as he jumped to the door.

"Hey, Osman! There's a dozen Bar C waddies headin' through the gap! Couldn't stop 'em in the dark without help —"

"Quick! Phil, take six men and git up in the woods. Make shore none of them hosses or steers wander down while they're here. Boys, keep hid now. I'll talk to these hombres. If they want trouble, we'll give it to 'em. If I raise my left arm up, go ahead and shoot 'em. And shoot to kill!"

Rapidly Osman's gunnies disposed themselves at points of vantage commanding the front of the rambling ranch house. Hard-faced devils, guns up, they manned various windows and chinks.

Al Osman, guns swinging at his bony hips, went out on the porch. He stood with his back to the shadowed wall.

Hardly were these dispositions made when a body of riders thudded over the log bridge. It drew to a sliding stop in front of the porch where Osman waited.

In the glow from the open door, Hatfield made out the foot-high brand on a horse — Bar C. In the lead was a young, reckless cowboy, not more than twenty or so. But he had steely blue eyes, and a strong chin bunched up his Stetson.

"Hey, Osman," he bawled. His voice banged like a shot against the wall.

"Who are yuh and what yuh want?" demanded Al Osman coldly, from the darkness.

"Oh, there yuh are! Yuh know me — Charlie Heidt of the Bar C. We want Fred Carlton. Hand him out or we'll come in and take him."

"We ain't seen Carlton," Osman snapped.

"He come over this way," declared Heidt, a leg slung up so he turned in his leather toward the ranch owner. "Yuh can't fool us, Osman. We know yore tricks."

"Tricks?" sneered Osman. "What yuh mean?"

"Gunnin' us in that gap, for one thing. And we're right close to guessin' how yore so-called syndicate stocks its range!"

"What! Why, yuh damn whippersnapper, don't talk to me like that!" roared Osman.

"That's the way to give it to him, Charlie," another waddy cried.

They were all young, impetuous, ready to defend their friends and spread to the last drop of blood.

"Yuh got it comin'," Heidt went on, the smile on his handsome lips belying the venom of his accusations. "Yuh're a traitor to us cowmen. I reckon yuh're helpin' them thievin' miners —"

"Shut up," broke in Osman angrily. "If the miners gun yuh in the gap, it ain't my fault. They don't shoot us, 'cause we got some brains in our heads."

"Yuh're workin' with 'em, that's why!" accused Heidt. "But I come here to git Fred Carlton. Pass him out. Give yuh jest ten seconds. One — Two —" He was counting, and counting fast.

Raw, hot-blooded war was here, fighting men tossing the lie in each other's teeth. A hundred guns, behind the thick house walls, pinned the dozen intrepid youths in the light circle. Heidt and his friends, unaware that Carlton had been taken by the sheriff, were throwing themselves in the face of death to save their pal . . .

"Yuh fool," shouted Osman, face flushed with angry blood. "Yuh're countin' yore own life out! The sheriff took Fred Carlton! Caught him red-handed, with stolen gold from them Pecos massacres!"

Jim Hatfield started. His heart quickened with great excitement of sudden discovery.

"How'd Osman savvy that?" he muttered, sure now that he was on the right trail.

But there was no time to think. Impatient at delay, Heidt was still counting. He had reached "Eight" when he suddenly realized the import of Osman's words. He stopped counting, with a gasp of rage.

"Why, yuh dirty, lyin' skunk!" he shouted.

Al Osman shifted. Hatfield saw the white patch that was his left hand starting to rise. That, the Ranger knew, was the signal. Instantly the covering gunnies would kill, wipe out the reckless youths in the yard —

The tall Ranger's blue-steel Colt flashed

into his slim hand. Scarcely seeming to take aim, Hatfield fired at the rising pale target. The crash of the heavy revolver startled the cowboys, and the gunmen hidden from sight.

Osman gave a screech of agony. He doubled up, holding his punctured left palm with his right hand.

"O — oo! O — oo!" he screamed.

Tender nerves had been shattered by the leaden slug. The wound tickled as maddeningly as it hurt.

"Ride, Heidt! Ride, yuh young fools," roared Hatfield. "Yuh're ambushed!"

The Ranger's stentorian command, ringing over the confused sounds, drove home to the waddies. Heidt and his pals snapped to quick action. Their indecision was jelled to certainty by Hatfield's shout. No one could hear the tall Ranger's voice in battle without a thrill. Decent hombres would rally around such a man, obey him as a leader.

Rifles were thrust through the windows of the house and out the doors. The gunnies swiftly came out of their surprise. The unexpected shot from the flank had temporarily stopped Al Osman's signal of death. Now they made ready to wipe out Heidt and his men.

"Hafta git into it," muttered Hatfield.

He swung to spatter six-gun bullets through the windows along the face of the rambling, long ranchhouse. He could see dark head-shapes in the openings, catch the glint of light on burnished gun barrels. He used both Colts, warming them up.

Roaring six-shooters blasted in the night. The flashes stabbed the dark where the Ranger crouched in gunfighter's stance. His wide shoulders were hunched, arms almost fully extended, boot heels dug in.

The terrible, deadly accuracy of this great fighting man, his muscles relaxed and action smooth as silk, was enough to strike fear into the hearts of an army of gunnies. Osman's killers felt lead tearing into them. It ripped holes in shoulders. Some took it in the head, keeled over to die. Others screamed with painful wounds. The rest sensed the winged death whirling past their ears. It showered splinters of wood and glass into their faces.

Al Osman rolled back inside the open door, among his followers. Yelling shrilly, cursing them, he ordered them to shoot down Heidt and his gang.

"Let 'em have it, damn yuh!" he shrieked.

Chapter IX
Welcome to
the A Bar O

A ragged volley rang out. Gun flares lighted the veranda with the fury of their explosions. Three of Charlie Heidt's boys crashed dead out of their leather seats. Others were nicked, including Heidt himself. But the Bar C men had already swung, thanks to Jim Hatfield's shrewd judgment. The instant given them by the Ranger guns had saved them from complete massacre. Under his fire, the gunnies could not concentrate to finish off the small party of cowboys.

Spurs dug in, Heidt's hombres pivoted. Their mustangs snorted, fighting the bits. But the expert riders handled them, whirled out of the light circle where they made easy targets.

"Give 'em some of their own medicine," bellowed Charlie Heidt.

He began to shoot back from the darkness, at the house. Six-shooters blazed away in the night. Slugs plugged into the house walls, tore through windows.

But they knew what they had to face now. They had more sense than to try a frontal attack on Al Osman's den. It teemed with killer guns. A hundred or more weapons, smacking at them, exposed the strength of the foe.

Stubbornly the Bar C cowboys retreated, shooting, howling their rage, threatening what they would do when they came back with reinforcements.

Reloading his Colts, Hatfield was left alone in the yard. Al Osman recovered his nerve as the worst pain eased from his smashed hand. He began yipping orders to his killers.

"Git out and go after 'em," he shouted. "The hombre that shot me is over there by the hoss corral. Go git him and fetch him here! I want to tear out his throat — Pronto, now, damn yore hides!"

Six-shooters gripped in horny hands, tough hombres spewed from the doors of the A Bar O ranch house. They were firing blind at the Ranger. Hatfield faded back around the wooden bars of the corral. Mustangs danced or ran about, startled by the heavy gunfire.

A shrill whistle sounded in a lull. A golden shape came flashing from the western shadows. Jim Hatfield hit leather without touching the metal of stirrup, as Goldy answered his call.

Men came running toward the horses, to take up pursuit of Heidt and his men — to shoot down the mysterious gunfighter who had hit Osman and spoiled the death trap.

"There he goes, over there!"

In the dim light they glimpsed him as he rode hell-for-leather around the corrals and headed along the western side of the house. Bullets sought him, hunted him. Osman was shrieking curses, egging his men on to take the horseman on the swift sorrel.

Hatfield swung in his saddle to shoot back and spoil their aim. Then he was past the corner, with the bulk of the building between himself and the mass of angry-eyed gunnies.

He had a minute before they could mount and start pursuit on horseback. The Ranger let the sorrel fly across the level space north of the house. No mustang could overtake Goldy in such a race. A bunched gang of riders swung the turn on his trail. But he rode through the darkness, allowing Goldy to pick the easiest way out.

For an hour they chased him. He outdistanced them, left them hunting blindly through the brakes and bushes. He turned east up the breast of the wooded mountains, and cut back.

"Mighty interestin' spot, the A Bar O," he remarked to the sorrel. "Oughta be a trail in here somewheres. Osman and his gang rode out from this direction."

Before long he found the trail, a beaten path through the pine woods. It wound in and out, and under the trees the shadows were black as ink. Goldy was lathered from the swift retreat. Hatfield let his pet take his time picking a way along the narrow road.

Presently he came to a spot that showed, through a leafy vista, the lighted ranch house in the distance. Goldy softly sniffed, giving his rider warning. Hatfield listened, his nostrils widening as he caught the soft breeze from the south.

"Huh! I know that smell, Goldy," he mused. It was the familiar odor of burnt hide and hair that came from branding.

A quarter mile down the winding trail, and he spotted the red glow of the fire through the trees. Leaving the sorrel, he stole through the pine woods toward the scene.

It was a large corral built in the woods, hidden from sight unless one came directly on it. Men were at work inside. Hatfield recognized Kansas Phil, Osman's aide. Phil was manipulating a running-iron, kneeling astride a big steer that bellowed with rage as the hot brand singed his hide.

There were a number of steers in the corral, divided into two bunches. As Hatfield crept in close, he could make out the foot-high brand on some — Bar C.

The string was untied and the animal Kansas Bill had worked on was allowed to heave himself up. As the beast struggled to its feet, Hatfield saw the A Bar O into which the Bar C had been worked with the running-iron.

"Easy enough," muttered the Ranger.

Such rustlers, he knew, would register a brand that could easily be run over marks belonging to some big outfit close to their theater of operations. The Bar crossed the A. With a stroke, the C finished to O.

The Ranger flattened as he heard a hail from the south, where stood the A Bar O house. Al Osman, left hand tied with a fresh bandage, rode up to the corral with several gunnies after him.

"What the hell happened?" demanded Kansas Phil, pausing in his brand-blotting. "I heard the shootin'. Did yuh finish 'em?"

"Most of 'em got clear," growled Osman. "Somebody plugged me through the hand.

Now, look. Hustle up these cows. Git 'em outa here 'fore it's light. Deliver 'em. I'm goin' to let them hosses loose and drive 'em way up into the woods. We got to have clean noses if Carlton and his army busts over here. He might fetch the sheriff along, and we want to look right."

"I'll be through here in another hour," promised Phil.

"I'll help yuh deliver the beef," Osman said. "The chief ain't gonna like this much, Kansas."

Kansas Phil went on with his branding. Osman left the corral with his men trailing him. They passed within a few yards of the hidden Ranger and broke east into the woods. After a time Hatfield heard them beating about, shooting and yelling. He faded back to the sorrel, mounted and cut over. Mustangs came dashing by him through the woods, chased from brush-corrals by the A Bar O men.

Hatfield swung north, riding with the flying horses. He reached out and caught one, slipped over to the animal's back. The beast was too tired to buck much. His hairy coat was matted with burrs and lather. Hatfield knew that this was one of the bunch Osman and his devils had ridden earlier that night.

The sorrel followed along as the Ranger brought the mustang to a stop. Quickly, match in cupped hand, he checked its brand — Bar C. Another he caught wore a Square 8, Sam Wills' brand.

"Reckon we've earnt a snooze," the Ranger told the sorrel.

Again mounted, he rode north. Drawing off into the forest, he rolled in his poncho and slept, while the keen-nosed gelding stood guard over his master.

He woke to the gray of dawn. A snack from saddle-bag and canteen and he was ready to go. Scouting the beaten trail, he picked up fresh cattle and shod horse tracks, heading north.

"Guess Osman and Kansas Phil're makin' that beef delivery," he murmured.

The tangy air of the pine woods widened his nostrils. Hatfield loved the wilds, with all its dangers. There were great compensations for the perils. As he gazed out over a mountain vista, he crooned a low tune to the handsome sorrel.

Still on the freshening sign, around noon Hatfield came up with a bunch of steers, driven by Al Osman, Kansas Phil and half a dozen gunnies. The beef cattle were being shoved down a slope dotted with the raw stumps of trees. Here was a great clearing in the wooded mountains. In the wide dip a large mining camp was built from virgin timber and whatever materials had been able to negotiate the steep slopes.

Hatfield sat at the edge of the forest, staring out over the Pecos Lady mine. The long barracks of raw-wood boards, curling as they dried in the sun, took the eye first of all. They were the dwellings of the numerous miners. Set apart from them a short distance were three smaller cabins, one marked "OFFICE."

North and west, the mountains rose in steep, breath-taking sweeps, pinnacles of gray and red rock gleaming in the sunlight. Smoke issued from the stone stack of a large outdoor furnace — evidently the smelter where ore was roughly melted down to portable form. A large pile of slag stood nearby. Instead of being thrown away, it was saved until the mine operators could get better facilities for further refining the ore.

The Pecos Lady was a good-sized mine, but it was just at the initial stage of its development. The inaccessibility of the region must first be overcome before it would pay in full. The opening of such a place was extremely expensive. Materials had to be brought long distances, apparatus erected. Up above, the mountain stream had been diverted into a great flume. Supported on wooden trestles, it brought water down to the long sluices, furnishing pressures for the big hoses at the lower end. There were small leaks here and there that spurted from cracks, showing the fierce pressure of the water.

The miners were operating on the eastern face of the mountain, throwing heavy streams from the nozzles against the earth. The water gullied the land, carrying with it topsoil, clay and smaller rocks, and leaving behind the heavy gold ore. Most of the water found its way back to the Sargent's natural course. But it turned the crystal-clear torrent into muddied, brownish-red liquid. As its speed declined near the Pecos, it gradually dropped the sediment.

Men in high leather boots and corduroy jackets were manipulating the nozzles, sending jets of water against the pitted earth. Others were shoveling crushed rock into barrows, delivering the loads to the smelter. Hatfield estimated that there were fifty or sixty men about.

In front of the office stood a huge, sloppy hombre whose bulbous red nose was a smeared blotch. He had on corduroy and a brown hat, and was watching the arrival of

Osman and the cows.

Having swept the site with his keen eyes, the Ranger trotted the golden gelding down the slope, skirting the tree stumps. On his vest was pinned the deputy sheriff badge furnished by Lew Barnes.

Al Osman, Red Ed Blucher and the gunny called Kansas Phil, turned aside to the office and dismounted. Evidently they meant to collect money from the manager. The others kept to their saddles. They swung the beeves west and drove them into a corral where the miners kept their meat on the hoof.

Blue-steel six-guns showing in his holsters, face serene and unruffled, Jim Hatfield cut past the sluices. He ducked his head as he pushed the sorrel underneath the flume on its X trestles. Then men at work glanced up and saluted him. His presence there did not seem to surprise the miners.

Quickly he rode the golden gelding up to the office. The bulbous-nosed manager glanced at him, nodded to the Ranger and turned back to Osman and his pals. Hatfield sat within a few feet of them, listening to their talk, taking in the manager.

"Okay, Morse. There's thirty head at eight dollars per," Osman was saying. "First-grade stock. Pay us."

Ted Morse, manager of the Pecos Lady in the field, nodded. He was a big fellow. His swollen nose with its broken red veins was the dominant feature of his face. His hand shook a little as he reached for a wallet. He began counting mine money in Osman's outstretched hand.

Jim Hatfield swung from his leather. The creak of the saddle caused Red Ed Blucher to turn. Blucher looked at him casually for an instant. When he recognized who it was, the carrot-topped gunny's mouth dropped wide. He swallowed a curse.

Blucher's startled exclamation made Al Osman swing and stare at the tall Ranger behind them. A greenish tinge passed across the sallow face of the A Bar O syndicate manager. His mouth, a gash in pock-marked cheeks, drew inward. Hatfield watched him with steely eyes, observed the yellow fear light Osman's close-set black eyes.

"He savvies who I am," thought the Ranger. "They think they're seein' a ghost!"

Chapter X
Hot Guns

Osman stayed frozen in his attitude. His punctured left hand was bandaged, but his right was free to go after the belted six-shooter at his hip. He did not try it though. Hatfield noted that Osman's uninjured hand was trembling at his side.

"What the hell's wrong?" growled Ted Morse. "Ain't this one of your men, Osman?"

Red Ed Blucher lost his head. His big paw, flecked with reddish hairs, flew to the black Colt hanging from his cartridge belt in an open-work holster. The florid face showed scabs and bruises where he had fallen in Eagleburg during his clash there with Hatfield.

Kansas Phil turned. He, too, knew the Ranger. Hatfield guessed that they all knew though they had believed him dead.

"Hold it —" began the Ranger.

But Red Ed was flustered.

The action came in speeding instant-fractions, too fast for the eye to follow. Blucher's .45 cleared leather, started to rise. The Ranger's draw, a trifle behind Blucher's, was coolly unerring, no unnecessary haste that would spoil aim. Hatfield was forced to shoot for a vital spot, with Red Ed's pistol coming up. Blucher was determined to have it out, then and there.

The officer's blue-steel Colt merged from oiled, supple socket, spoke as Blucher's echoed it. The redhead's slug nipped a chunk from Hatfield's boot toe, spread wide from its mate. The huge Blucher stood a moment, teetering on spidery legs that were bowed to horse's ribs. Then his arm dropped limp. The gun fell from his relaxed fingers. He lurched heavily against Al Osman and would have gone down. But the A Bar O manager caught him in his unhurt right arm.

"Damn yuh! Yuh've kilt him!" yelled Kansas.

Red Ed Blucher's promising career as a murderer and gunman was over. Now he was only a sagging length of flesh and bone, carrion for the vultures that suddenly wheeled high above the mountain crags.

Ted Morse cursed, his voice falsetto in excitement. His eyes were wide in alarm as he stared into the round black hole of Hatfield's deadly Colt. It fascinated him as a snake's eye fascinates a bird.

"Don't — don't shoot," he stammered.

Hatfield kept an eye on Kansas Phil. The desperado had his hands free, but he made no attempt to fight. The lightning speed of the tall Ranger awed him. He dared not move a muscle. Osman let go of the heavy Blucher. His prime consideration was what Hatfield meant to do next. The dead ambusher rolled to a stop on the rough dirt.

Echoing in the mountain gulch, the shots electrified the Pecos Lady workers. Miners dropped picks, shovels, and hoses, snatched up rifle and pistols waiting at hand. They started running toward the office. Osman's drivers had guided the stolen cows into the butterfly gate of the corral. Now they shut the bars and swung their horses.

Jim Hatfield had looked over many of the miners back in Eagleburg. He had judged the rank-and-file as honest if rough men. He knew that to pacify the district across the Pecos he must first show them the truth and enlist them solidly behind him.

Deliberately he shifted his position. He placed his back against the log wall of the office, near the open door. Men's eyes closely followed every move he made.

"Who — who are you, mister?" asked Ted Morse. "A — a sheriff?" He had seen the badge on Hatfield's vest.

"Deputy, one of Lew Barnes' from Eagleburg. I reckon yuh're Morse, field manager of this mine."

"Yeah, I am. But — What's the meanin' of killin' Blucher that way, if you're a lawman?"

"Blucher's a rustler and a drygulcher, Morse. That beef Osman sold yuh belongs to the Bar C and other ranchers east of here. The brands have been run over."

"I wouldn't know about that. They look okay to me, mister. We've bought cows for beef right along from Osman." He frowned at the manager of the A Bar O Syndicate. "Is this true, Osman? You've stolen cows from the ranchers? We wanted to avoid such trouble all along."

Osman glanced over his shoulder, an appraising look to see how close his men were. They were hurrying to back him up. A large number of miners also crowded toward the office — armed men who would fight for Ted Morse. Bearded faces scowled at the Ranger as they awaited orders.

Morse looked from Osman's sneering face to Hatfield's calm features. Hatfield was fully at ease. Every man there felt awe of the great fighting machine that was the Ranger.

But it was more than his ability with six-guns that had caused Captain McDowell to dispatch him. He was a diplomat as well as a warrior. He knew how to sway a crowd.

"He lies, Morse," Osman snarled. "That's syndicate beef we sold yuh."

"Gents," began the Ranger, voice carrying clearly to all the miners. "Yuh've been annoyed plenty up here and I don't blame yuh for being riled. But the ranchers have reason for bein' sore, too. Osman's been stealin' their beef and hosses, takin' pot-shots at line riders, and layin' it on you."

"Is that right, mister?" cried a big miner. "Why, damn yuh, Osman, I'll —"

"Hold it," ordered Hatfield. "I'm here to bring Law to this country. Osman's my prisoner. Unbuckle yore gunbelt and let her drop, Osman."

Al Osman licked his thin lips. He hunted with his eyes for support from the miners. But he found none in the angry, reddened faces glaring at him. Threats were growled in bearded throats. Now that sentiment had turned against them, Osman's gunnies quailed before the calm Ranger and the growing rage of the men they had deceived.

With his uninjured right hand, Osman slowly unbuckled his gun belt. He let it fall around his booted ankles. When he stepped from the loop, he sneered at the tall Ranger.

"Okay — okay, deputy. We'll see who comes right side up at the end!"

As Osman's guns fell, the quartet of gunnies coming from the corral saw how things stood. They jerked on their reins and swung, galloping away in a fury of hoofs. Hatfield's Colt brought one down, nicked another. Miners fired after the running men. But three managed to make the woods and disappeared.

The flare-up subsided. Osman shouted hoarsely:

"Yuh damn fools! This feller's a spy for the cowmen, gents! They're the ones been raidin' yore gold trains and shootin' down yore pals! I tell yuh Sheriff Barnes jest arrested Fred Carlton. That's the son of John Carlton of the Bar C. Caught him redhanded with some of the Pecos Lady gold! What more proof do yuh want?"

Hatfield took a step toward the sneering, sallow-faced gunman chief. Osman shrank, yellow fear flashing across his dark eyes. Hatfield had picked Osman as a coward. The man hated the Ranger, but he was more afraid of him than anything else.

"Is that right, deputy?" demanded Ted Morse, his voice thick with emotion. "Did Barnes catch Carlton?"

"Yeah. It shows the Law 'll give yuh justice, men. If Carlton's guilty, which ain't proved yet, he'll be punished —"

Hatfield was fighting to maintain his hold on the miners. Osman's information had startled them. It made them certain that their cowmen enemies were murderous killers with whom they could not deal, save by force.

"You must be crazy," Ted Morse interrupted fiercely. "Comin' up here an' sayin' the ranchers're innocent! Why, Lew Barnes has proved 'em guilty."

"Carlton claims he was tricked, framed! I checked his story and the trail leads to Osman. Take a look at the brands on those cows the A Bar O jest drove in. Yuh'll see they're fresh run, over the Bar C —"

The sound of shooting stopped the Ranger as he fought to convince these miners. The firing from the eastern flank of the mountain rapidly increased. The men above could look down and see figures struggling through the woods and brush, keeping up a running scrap with mounted cowboys who pursued them.

"It's our men, Roberts and Potter. And there's John Carlton after 'em!" bawled Ted Morse. "Hustle, boys! We've got to save 'em!"

A trail wound down the steep mountain, the road to the east and far-off civilization. A hot sun burned on the bloody scene of conflict, a major clash in which scores of men would die. The miners who had been listening to Jim Hatfield leaped to assist their pals. Evidently John Carlton and his ranchers had been so infuriated that they were making a frontal attack. Clearly, they meant to wipe out the Pecos Lady once and for all.

Face purple with excited fury, Ted Morse moved with surprising speed for his size. He lumbered swiftly after his fighters.

Hatfield took a moment in which to drive Osman and Kansas Phil into the office and snap the padlock on the oak door. Then he leaped on Goldy's back and spurred after Morse. Now he could hear the fierce shouts of ranchers and miners. The gunfire swelled to great volume as more of Morse's hombres hustled into the fray.

Instead of heading directly toward the scene of the running fight, Ted Morse turned south toward a pile of red rocks. As he came abreast of the boulders, Hatfield

116

saw that the huge manager held a box of matches in one fat hand. In the other he held a lighted match that he had just struck. Morse must be at the end of a fuse, leading to a buried powder mine. There would naturally be explosives at the Pecos Lady. The miners must have set the trap against just such an attack as was now occurring.

A quick bullet from the Ranger's Colt spattered lead and rock fragments into Morse's eyes. With a howl of pain, the manager fell back. The lighted match was still in his fingers.

"Come outa that!" roared Hatfield, spurring toward the rocks.

He couldn't see Morse now, for the manager was low behind the jagged boulders. But he caught sight of the blue-yellow sparks of a fuse train running through a tunnel in the rocks.

Then Ted Morse bobbed up, shot at him with a revolver. The sloppy hombre's hand was unsteady. The bullet missed by a yard. The blue-steel Ranger Colt flared again. Morse dropped out of sight.

Hatfield had no time to check on the manager. He swerved the sorrel toward the last point where he had seen the sparking fuse. The fuse was covered with rocks and narrow boards to protect it throughout its length. It was by quick perception of this that he traced its course.

Hitting the rough ground, the Ranger ripped aside stones and timber. He found the gray fuse, caught the fire as it rapidly ran through — and broke the train!

He straightened, swinging to the golden sorrel again. A bullet bit a chunk from his thigh, half whirled him around. The shot came from above.

Al Osman and Kansas Phil had escaped from the office shack. They were running toward their horses.

Hatfield's answering bullets sent Kansas Phil crashing to the dirt. The hombre leaped to his feet again a moment later, ran on limping. Osman jumped behind a building, out of the Ranger's sight. Hatfield had no time to pursue them. The ranchers were pushing up the mountain, hot on the heels of the miners. Now they were close to meeting the reinforcements from the mine.

He rode the sorrel across the rough ground, keeping the fuse line in view. Bullets whistled over him, plugged into the ground. The banging of rifles and pistols tore the fragrant air of the wilderness viciously, the hot sun lit the scene of blood.

Into the mêlée of leaden death the Ranger rode, seeing the twisted, furious faces of fighting miners. They had joined the party from Eagleburg, led by George Potter and David Roberts. With them were only a few of the mules and horses that had composed the pack train. On the backs of the surviving animals were roped wounded miners.

Hatfield spurred up to Potter and Roberts, chiefs of the miners. They were dust-covered, limping, their bearded faces strained.

Potter stared up into the grim face of the Ranger.

"Attacked, damn them! Shot at us all the way from town, deputy!"

Roberts was furious, cursing the cowmen, shaking his fist at them. Hatfield glimpsed the tall figure of John Carlton as the giant rancher whooped his men on to the attack.

"Morse! Set off that powder mine — they're right over it! Stop them!"

"Pull yore men up to the mine, Potter. Stop shootin'. I'll handle Carlton," the Ranger ordered.

"You're crazy," snarled Potter. "They picked off our mules and horses at long range. I recognized Carlton, Wills and their pals."

Roberts seized the Ranger's spurred boot, shook it, looking up into Hatfield's cool gray-green eyes. His own were blazing. A civilized, middle-aged man, David Roberts had now become a raving devil, crying for blood revenge.

"Last night they attacked us! Killed half a dozen, wounded plenty more. Is there no law in this land, damn you!"

"Stop yore men shootin'," roared Hatfield. "I'll go down and talk to Carlton — Pronto, now!"

Bullets were ripping up at them, cutting the dirt, shrieking in the dry air of the mountains.

Gasping, cursing men, showing the terrible effects of the long running battle from Eagleburg to the Pecos Lady, stumbled blindly up the slope. The tall Ranger spurred the golden sorrel down, oblivious to the rain of lead that threatened to finish him.

At the first volleys from the reinforcements, sent by Ted Morse from the Pecos Lady site, the ranchers had paused. They rode back and forth, shooting from their saddles. But as Potter and Roberts led their exhausted followers up, John Carlton and Sam Wills uttered the shrill cowboy whoop, urged their men to a final charge. There were around a hundred armed cowmen in the party. They were dominated by John Carlton's tall figure.

Hatfield could think only of the fact that he must stop before it was too late.

Jim Hatfield, McDowell's star Ranger, had been in many a ticklish spot carrying the law of Texas to the frontiers. This was the man who had smashed the Gunsmoke Empire on the Rio. He had rid the Southwest of the most vicious outlaw of all time in Peril Rides the Pecos. He had outwitted and outfought powerful Panhandle Bandits. Now he balanced on a ticklish scale. Only the weight of a hair one way or the other would decide the difference between life and death, between Law and Chaos.

Hand raised high over his Stetson in a gesture of peace, the Ranger rode straight toward the raging, blood-thirsty ranchers.

CHAPTER XI
COLT LAW

They recognized the tall Ranger on the magnificent golden sorrel. For the second time Jim Hatfield calmly went between the warring factions of the land.

John Carlton rode to meet him, waving his men to stop. They sat their lathered, panting mustangs. But they spent the precious minutes reloading their hot guns. Their faces under the Stetsons were grim and triumphant.

John Carlton's hawklike features were awry with a mixture of rage and inner torture. He had several bleeding flesh wounds, but he was not the sort to show physical hurt. It was mental anguish that made his eyes burning pools of unhappiness.

"No use to try to stop us this trip, deputy."

Sam Wills, Elsie's father and owner of the Square 8, growled agreement with his old friend's declaration.

"We're goin' to wipe them dirty skunks off the earth, here and now," went on Carlton, teeth gritting. "Git outa the way, less yuh want to take bullets."

Hatfield blocked the giant rancher's path. The spot where the bunched cowmen sat their horses was a small clearing which had been cut around the trail to the Pecos Lady. The Ranger noted the loose rocks and dirt under the sorrel's dancing hoofs.

Withdrawing up the mountain, the miners had not stopped shooting. But the range was longer. Bullets thudded into the ground a hundred yards in advance of the ranchers.

"Yuh're breakin' the Law of Texas, Carlton," Hatfield told the big fellow gravely.

Carlton gave a bitter laugh. "Law! Yuh call it Law when yore sheriff arrests my son on a trumped-up charge of murder?"

That was it, thought Hatfield. Word had come through to the Bar C that Lew Barnes had taken Fred Carlton. His father's reaction had been to blame it on the miners.

"Sheriff took yore son in one of yore line shacks. He found some of the stolen gold in there with him."

John Carlton's flush deepened under his tanned hide.

"I reckon yuh're with yore chief, Sheriff Barnes, deputy."

"C'mon, boss. Let's go up and git 'em," growled a young cowhand around a cigaret that drooped nonchalantly from his boyish mouth. "Shove that dumb sheriff outa the way and let's ride!"

Hatfield glanced at the speaker. It was Charlie Heidt, the reckless devil who had led a handful of men against the A Bar O.

"Hold tight to yore shirt, Heidt," drawled the Ranger. "Yuh'll lose it shore otherwise. Mebbe yuh better try countin' ten again, 'fore yuh go off half-cocked."

Heidt jumped, stared hard at the unruffled officer. A flush reddened the boyish cheeks.

"How — Who the hell told yuh that?"

Another young cowboy, who had been with Heidt that night, cursed in amazement.

"Say, that's the jigger give us such a hand at the A Bar O! Thought his voice was familiar. When I was crossin' the bridge I looked back and saw his face when he fired at Osman's gunnies. Now I know him!"

"Yuh're an all-fired smart deputy, mister," growled John Carlton suspiciously. "Yuh seem to know a hell of a sight more than anybody else 'bout what goes on round these parts."

Sam Wills stirred in his leather, pushing high in his stirrups.

"Say, what the hell's Roberts up to? Funny lookin' fire there —"

Hatfield looked over his shoulder. David Roberts was running up past the rocks where the Ranger had stopped Ted Morse from blowing the cowmen to bits. Near the office stood George Potter and Ted Morse. Evidently Morse had not been badly wounded, for he had rejoined his pals. Groups of miners were watching the ranchers, catcalling at them, firing a shot now and again.

It was the leaping spark of the powder train that Sam Wills had glimpsed. Hatfield saw the faint trace of smoke over the rapidly moving fire.

"Hustle! Turn and ride," he roared. "Yuh'll be blowed to hell in a minute if yuh sit here! Ground's mined!"

Driving the startled cowmen before him, he spurred down the slope. Rather than attempt to check the explosion again, he preferred that the dangerous powder mine go off. He knew it was the crazed David Roberts who had crept to the fuse end while Hatfield palavered with John Carlton.

Panicked by the menace they could not face as they did gunfire, the cowmen rode the rough east trail. They slid their horses, skidded on shale and loose dirt.

The terrific detonation slewed Goldy around. Flattened against the sorrel's body, Hatfield was nearly torn from his seat. Several cowboys went down, mounts shocked to their knees. Sound shattered the air. The earth rumbled and shook. Dazed men gripped manes and leather.

A dense cloud of smoke and rubble rose majestically in the air. The space where the ranchers had stood a few minutes before was now a jagged, smoking crater. A rain of clod and stones spattered the leaves like thick hail.

Hatfield's swift action had saved them from serious injury. More than that, he had saved the range. Many of the district leaders were in the crowd. Their death would have meant an end to several cow country dynasties. Broken widows would have sold out for a song to get away from the tragic country. Sons and relatives, who had lost their loved ones, would have sworn a blood feud to the end against the Pecos Lady. The one slim chance Jim Hatfield had of bringing peace to the land would have gone up in the smoke with shattered bodies.

Ears still roaring and ringing with the noise, men stared at each other, wiping cold sweat from stained faces. Young Charlie Heidt began cursing in a high-pitched, unnatural voice. The others were too stunned to speak.

Jim Hatfield alone had prevented the final wiping out of both factions fighting across the Pecos. Single-handed, the Ranger sought to hold whatever advantage his keen brain and swift guns had afforded him. But powerful, hidden forces sought to balk him. His death would mean success to them and the end of the decent men he must save.

With his genius at getting to the root of evil, Hatfield had dug out evidence against Al Osman and his A Bar O. But he was sure that others, higher up, controlled the syndicate's criminal moves. The syndicate was the sort of outfit which would absorb the range. It would steal and slay to gain control.

Yet there was more in it than simply the increasingly valuable rangeland owned by Carlton, Wills and their friends. Complicated by the Pecos Lady, whose inherent value Hatfield knew, and which he must save for the innocent back in Austin, the problem taxed the Ranger's ingenuity.

He wanted a little time and freedom of hand in which to work. But at each step he was forced to turn aside to prevent the very citizens he had sworn to protect from being annihilated.

"Osman's the one I want," he thought, even as he shook himself together and swung once more on John Carlton. "He's yeller, inside that sneerin' hard shell he puts on for a front."

He spoke aloud to Carlton, loud enough for the others to hear.

"Yuh'll never git up that mountain, Carlton. They've got powder stored there. They can throw bombs at yuh. Besides, they could pick yuh off from the buildin's 'fore yuh reached them."

The explosion had shocked some sense back into the cowmen. The miners were whooping, shooting ineffectively, daring them to charge again.

"Boss," growled Charlie Heidt, "thing to do is leave them skunks till later. We'll git 'em some dark night if they ain't had enough. I'm in favor of rescuin' Fred, pronto."

There was muttered approbation.

"Yuh let Fred stay right where he is," the Ranger said. "He's safe in jail. The Law will take its course."

"S'pose them polecats lie and say Fred raided them gold trains and massacred the drivers?" demanded Carlton. "We never did that, deputy. None of us're thieves or killers. It wasn't till them miners deviled us so far that we begun shootin' in earnest."

"Yuh've been a lawman," insisted Hatfield, his gray-green eyes intent on the big rancher. "Uphold it now, Carlton."

"As yuh was sayin', Boss," drawled Charlie Heidt, "seems to me this hombre is right pert for a deputy! Who the hell does he think he is, tellin' us what to do?"

The moment had come! Slowly, as the eyes of the ranchers grew hostile, the tall Ranger reached inside his shirt to the secret pocket. He raised his slim hand above his head. The stained bandage in his black hair attested how close he had come to death in his lone fight for these very men who now questioned him.

All eyes sought the silver star on silver circle.

"A Texas Ranger!" cried John Carlton.

It did the trick. Few as the Rangers were, each one counted for an army of local deputies. Texans respected them, knew that only the most rigid justice would be dealt out by these hard-shooting, fair and square officers. Men looked to them for help in desperate straits.

"My name's Jim Hatfield, from Austin.

Yuh might as well know. The others seem to."

Charlie Heidt was silenced. John Carlton stuck out his big hand, shook with Hatfield.

"Mighty glad to savvy jest who yuh are, Hatfield. And — I'll do what yuh say."

"C'mon, then. We'll ride to yore ranch."

The battered party of cowmen swung eastward and headed for the Bar C.

There was little, the Ranger figured, that he could do until the country calmed down a bit. His main idea was to get his hands on Al Osman. Then he would know how to use the fear he had generated in the sneering boss of the A Bar O Syndicate. To do that, he would need the cover of darkness. As yet he was not ready to round up Osman's horde of gunnies.

It was late afternoon when they walked their horses across the bridge over Sargent Creek. They pulled up before the great Bar C house. The cowboys turned their horses into corrals, then walked with their stiff, bow-legged stride toward the bunkhouse and a hot meal. Hatfield went inside the house with John Carlton and Sam Wills.

A pretty girl with full red lips, anxious eyes, came to meet them. She kissed Wills, and asked eagerly:

"Have you any more news of Fred?"

Wills shook his head. The stout man was worn out. Elsie gave a cry of alarm as she noticed the dried blood on her father's arm.

"It ain't nuthin' but a scratch," Wills said. "Elsie, I want yuh to meet Ranger Jim Hatfield. He saved us from bein' blowed to mincemeat."

The young woman smiled up, but it was a wan smile. She was worried about her sweetheart, Fred Carlton.

The Chinese cook was hastily preparing a hot meal. Jim Hatfield felt he certainly could stand one. The tall Ranger looked curiously at the old-style cap-and-ball Colts crossed on the wall. The filigree of gold in the walnut handles was cunningly wrought. They were beautifully made weapons, expensive in their day.

Sam Wills came over and stood by Hatfield.

"Those belonged to Cimarron Jones, Ranger. Yuh know Carlton was chief of vigilantes in Abilene, back in Kansas, years ago. Cimarron Jones was one mean sidewinder, a bandit who ran a big gang of killers up there. John got him, though — shot it out with him and his lieutenants."

"Looks like a bullet hit that cylinder," remarked Hatfield, indicating the slight dent in the metal.

"Yuh're right. One of Carlton's last slugs tore the end off'n Jones' little finger. It was a great fight, aw right. Cimarron was tough, but John was tougher and brought him out."

"Dead?"

"No, sir. Stunned and wounded, but alive. Sent him to prison for life."

"Come gettum," shouted the Chinaman, with a broad grin on his yellow moonlike face.

Chapter XII
Luring Retreat

After dinner Hatfield spoke privately with John Carlton. He obtained the rancher's solemn promise not to make any more attacks until he heard from the Ranger.

Saddling up the rested sorrel, Hatfield crossed the bridge and galloped westward for the A Bar O.

It was early morning when he approached the gap that led to the syndicate's headquarters. Starting up across the mountain shoulder as he had done before, he stopped as the first grayness of dawn lighted the eastern sky. It was cool, and a west wind funneled through the ravine. To his keen ears came the sound of hundreds of hoofs echoing up from the rocky trail below.

Swinging, he looked down across the wide stretch of rangeland. Out of the gap dark figures of horsemen swept, squad after squad. He estimated that there were over a hundred gunnies in the gang. It was the A

Bar O, and they headed north in the rising light.

The distance was too great to recognize individuals. But obviously they were heading for some mischief.

"Mebbe I kin cut Osman outa that bunch," he mused.

Leading the sorrel, he turned and worked back the way he had come.

The trail of the band of killers was easy for the Ranger to follow. Dust still hung in the air. The shod hoofs had marked the shifting alkali. He stayed back, out of sight, seeking mesquite clumps, rocks and buttes, the swelling of the foothills.

This led him at an angle away from the rugged mountains in which lay the Pecos Lady. Northeast, miles from the gap, he could look down across a stretch of badlands and see the mass of riders ahead. Faces were blurred by bandanna masks.

Then he saw the ragged line of men approaching from the west. Many of them were walking, others had horses. They were straggling along, heading east for Eagleburg.

The entire force of the Pecos Lady mine moved across the upheaved hell of rocks, interspersed by giant cacti and thorned bushes. Within half an hour, the miners would come to the blind gap through which the trail must run. There would be the A Bar O gunnies, horses concealed behind them.

"So that's the way they done it," muttered the Ranger.

Hurriedly he spurred on, the golden sorrel running full-tilt north. Dust billowed up under the flashing hoofs as the tall Ranger hastened to smash the ambush.

He unshipped his Winchester, for this was a long-range job. Within rifle shot, the van of miners close to the gap. The Ranger halted the sorrel, jumped to a flat rock from which he could shoot with protection. He began dropping long bullets into the crouched gunnies lining the lip of the pass.

His first one kicked up the shale a foot behind a burly masked hombre. Now that he had the range, he shot again before the man could shift, saw him fold up in a ball. The crack of the Winchester was faint against the wind. Before the surprised gunmen guessed what went on, Hatfield had plugged lead into two more.

"Sorta spoils their game," he muttered, aiming again at the form of a squatted killer.

They were turning in alarm at the mysterious fire from their rear. Above them, the Ranger had them where they could not take cover from his bullets. Next time he shot, they located him by the smoke puff from the rifle. Half a dozen jumped for their horses and started toward his position.

The noise of the Ranger's rifle caused the miners to stop, seize their weapons and make ready to defend themselves. They were dismounting, scattering into the rocks. The gunnies fired a volley that sought them in vain. The miners returned the lead with interest.

The six who had detached themselves to take care of the Ranger were now five. Before they were within pistol shot, Hatfield had shot one from his mustang. Colt bullets were rapping against the breast of the Ranger's rock, singing in the warming air about his Stetson.

Coolly he took aim. Another gunny slewed off, rolled from his saddle and crashed on the rocky slope. Accurate as death, the Ranger shot to kill. He was aware that the worst of the trouble between ranchers and miners had been fomented, and he also knew by whom. The .30-30 bullet from the Ranger's hot Winchester flashed invisible to the bulky body of a masked devil in the lead. The man's mustang turned aside. The corpse banged along the ground, one leg caught in a stirrup, until the horse stopped running.

Appalled by his deadly aim, the surviving three, one of them with a smashed shoulder from Ranger lead, ceased their charge. They jerked around the reins. Howling in baffled fury, they rode back to their mates. Hatfield got another between the shoulder-blades and returned him dead in his leather to his friends.

Bursts of gunfire rattled below. Hatfield was putting long-range slugs into the exposed killers. The stinging death he dealt broke their desire to destroy the miners. In their fierce hearts a single hatred flamed. They had to finish off the rifleman above who had ruined their murderous game.

With one accord the horde of gunnies jumped for their horses. Mounted, hoarse shouts rising in their bearded throats, their eyes gleaming red hatred over the masks, they pounded up at Jim Hatfield.

"Don't see Al Osman," he murmured, sliding back from the top of the slanted flat boulder.

He whistled and the golden sorrel flashed up to the rear of the rock. He hit leather in a leap, clamped his powerful legs around Goldy's ribs.

"Run, Goldy," he ordered. "And don't step in no gopher holes!"

He drew off south, the raging mob after him.

Fred Carlton sat on the hard wooden bench of Eagleburg jail, chin in hands. Used to the free air of the open range, such confinement was torture to him. The uncertainty of his plight, the terrible accusation against him, did not help his peace of mind.

After a slow, roundabout trip to town, under the posse's guns, had been locked in the small jail by Lew Barnes and left to stew in his own juice.

Shame depressed him. He knew he was innocent, but everybody seemed to think he was guilty. They were not surprised, either. They considered it natural that the cowmen should have committed the crimes against the miners in revenge.

"What'll Elsie think?" he kept asking himself.

After two days of this, he was fit to be tied. Lew Barnes, though sadly sympathetic, only shook his head when Fred protested his innocence.

"Mebbe I shouldn't blame yuh, boy," the sheriff said miserably. "Yuh're young and hot-headed. It's up to the judge and jury now, though."

Fred gave up trying to convince Barnes.

That evening the sheriff fetched him his supper, and gave him fresh water. Fred finally lay down on his hard board bunk, and managed to fall into a troubled sleep.

He woke with a start. The moon was streaming in through the bars at the back of the cell. Something small thudded by him. Another object stung the flesh of his face. He realized that they were pebbles, flung through the window. Instantly he was up, alert. He sprang to the bars, looked out.

"Fred!" The whisper came from a shadow at the side.

"Hello, Charlie. That you?" Carlton, heart leaping, had recognized young Charlie Heidt's voice.

"Yeah, we're takin' yuh out, Fred. Is the sheriff asleep?"

Fred tiptoed over to the door, looked through the bars. He listened intently and heard heavy snoring. Lew Barnes was sleeping in the outer room of the little lockup.

"Okay, Charlie!" he called back softly to his friend.

A heavy crowbar was inserted between the window bars. Three more shadows flitted in the moonlight behind the jail. They were young riders of the Bar C, cronies of Charlie Heidt. They put their weight on the lever and heaved. The bar against which they shoved groaned in its deep cement socket. The first one sprang from its base without too much noise. But it was necessary to break out another before Fred could get through the opening. Hastily the cowboys started on this. The steel creaked. Suddenly the second bar gave way, much more easily than the first had. Heidt and his pals lost their balance and sprawled on the ground. The crowbar fell against the wall with a terrific clatter.

As Fred Carlton started to climb through the gap, he heard Lew Barnes cry out:

"What the hell's goin' on out there!"

The sheriff came to the cell door, peeked through the bars. With an oath he saw Fred's legs disappearing out the window.

Charlie Heidt seized Carlton's shoulders, dragged him free.

"Fetch them hosses, Vern," Heidt whispered hoarsely.

They ran around the jail. Lew Barnes had come out on the porch, six-shooter in hand.

"Halt," the sheriff bawled. "Halt or I'll fire!"

The mustangs galloped up, led by two more of Fred's friends. The young fellows forked their horses, swung to gallop down the plaza to freedom. But Lew Barnes' Colt barked, and a bullet sang within inches of them.

"The old goat," Heidt growled.

Before Fred could stop him, the wild young fellow yanked his iron and shot back at the sheriff. No more bullets came from Barnes.

"Yuh fool. Yuh hit him!" gasped Fred.

"Aw, I didn't mean to," protested Charlie. "Jest meant to scare him, Fred."

Grimly Carlton rode on with his mates. The shots had roused the town. But long before any action could be taken, the gang was out in the chaparral, streaking for home.

Next morning, the sun golden in an azure sky, the six were far west of Eagleburg.

"Somebody comin'," growled Heidt.

The hot-blooded waddy had lost a lot of fire since the shooting of the sheriff. Everybody had liked Lew Barnes, had known he was in sympathy with the cowmen.

They drew off the dusty trail into the chaparral, waiting to see who might be approaching. Accompanied by Elsie and Sam Wills and twenty riders, John Carlton swung the bend. Fred Carlton stepped his lathered horse out into the trail.

"Mornin', Dad," he said. Then his voice broke. "Elsie —"

The girl pushed her horse to him. Relief

flooded her face at sight of him.

"Fred! They've let you go."

His father's lined, grim face softened.

"Say, that Ranger shore works fast. Did he talk Lew Barnes into freein' yuh, son?"

"No, Dad. Charlie and the boys took me outa jail."

The whole unhappy tale was drawn from the reluctant lips of the rescuers. John Carlton listened, his face showing no emotion, until the end. His eyes were stern as he swung on his son, whom he loved above life itself.

"Yuh've got to go back," he said. "Turn and ride."

"No — no!" Elsie cried.

Her father frowned at her. She bit her lip, looking from the stern faces of the older men to the defiant young ones.

"I've give my word," John Carlton said slowly, "and I mean to keep it, son. Yuh're not guilty. The Law'll clear yuh of attackin' and stealin' from the miners. What's happened to Barnes is somethin' else. I'm sorry yuh disobeyed my orders, Heidt. And I'm sorry that yuh saw fit to leave the jail with him, Fred. I was afeared of somethin' like this."

"Dad," growled Fred, "I can't stand bein' shut up in that jail."

Anger waved over him, but he held down his surging rebellion. It was a hard decision to make.

At last Fred swung his mustang and faced east for Eagleburg. Elsie pushed her horse beside his, glanced fearfully into the stalwart youth's bitter, set face.

"Your father's right, Fred. It is the only way."

She reached out a hand to him. Holding it, he nodded. Now he felt stronger and better.

"Okay, Boss," Heidt growled. "If Fred goes, I go too."

He rode into line, and his pals trailed after him.

The run to Eagleburg was an unhappy, tense time for all. If Lew Barnes had been killed, then there was no way out for them.

They came in through the bush, down the slope toward the little settlement. The town seemed deserted. It was middle afternoon and the sun was hot. Everybody who could, was indoors where there was shade.

The little lockup from which Heidt had snatched Fred Carlton stood wide open. They could see the smashed window at the back, the steel bars bent and protruding from the adobe wall. The party from the Bar C rode to the jail, but it was empty.

CHAPTER XIII
RESCUE!

Silently they swung and headed for the Bull's Head, the big central saloon. They quickly dismounted and ran up on the porch.

Fred strode by his giant dad's side. Their faces were grim as they came to face the music. Young Carlton hit the batwings and pushed through to the cooler interior. The odor of damp sawdust and liquor met them. For a moment they could not see clearly because of the brilliant light outside.

"Well, doggone my hide!" a rough voice bellowed from down the bar.

Fred Carlton sighed with deep relief. Elbow crooked, finishing a tall drink, Sheriff Lew Barnes stood hale and hearty.

John Carlton's craggy face wreathed in a smile. He strode down the big room, hand out to the lean sheriff.

"Never was so glad to see a man drinkin' afore, Lew! Have a couple on the Bar C."

Lew Barnes was scowling at Charlie Heidt and Fred.

"Yuh young rapscallions! Look what yuh done!" He pointed to the lump, hen's-egg size, on the side of his head. "Bullet yuh fired glanced off'n a spike and stunned me, dang yuh. Yuh're goin' to be fined for shootin' off firearms in town, or I ain't sheriff of this county."

"They'll git what's comin' to 'em," promised John Carlton. "I've brought the boy back, Lew. He's yore prisoner and he won't run away again."

"Thanks, John. Sorry I hadda bring him in but he was caught red-handed."

Lew Barnes reached in his pocket, brought out a bunch of keys.

"Here's the keys to the lockup, Fred. Yuh kin let yourself in."

Fred Carlton took the keys, turned and left the room. Elsie met him and walked across the plaza with him. She went inside the jail and kissed him. Then she sat down outside the broken cell.

An hour passed. The sun was dropping lower in the brazen sky. Shouts and scattered shots came from the northwest. Elsie went out on the porch to see what was coming. She hurried back to Fred Carlton.

"Miners from the Pecos Lady, Fred.

Eighty or ninety of them. They look all done in."

"Huh. S'pose they'll say we done it," Carlton replied bitterly.

He stood up on a bench and looked out the little window as far as he could crane. Across the plaza came a bunch of men, van of the retreating miners. Ted Morse, the heavy-faced manager; David Roberts, expert observer and close friend of Anson Elms, president of the company; George Potter, who had been sent from Austin to check up on the war and trouble, all rode lathered, weary horses. There were wounded men on burros. About half had mounts. The rest footed it.

They were dry, panting for water. There was a stampede for the big horse troughs along the edge of the plaza. Exhausted men threw themselves down on the grass after drinking. The animals had to be restrained from killing themselves with too much liquid.

Sheriff Lew Barnes came from the Bull's Head and hustled to the distressed party of miners. Eyes wild, several days' beard on his stained, scratched face, David Roberts cried out:

"Sheriff, we've just escaped with our lives!

Cowmen attacked us again, shot us up. We ran out of food and water. Damn Texas! I'm leavin' here and I'll never go back to the Pecos Lady."

Ted Morse and George Potter echoed Roberts' furious sentiments.

"You're one hell of a lawman," growled Roberts. "Law! There's none across the Pecos."

"I'm doin' the best I kin," muttered Barnes, as he looked over the bearded, distressed faces of the miners. None had shaved for many days. Thorns had torn the flesh of their cheeks and ripped their clothing. Some had scabbed-over bullet creases. "I'm sure tryin' to bring peace, gents."

"Peace!" exclaimed Roberts in disgust. "I know where to find that, and I'm going back to civilization. If anybody's fool enough to go into those mountains again, let them go. Not for me."

"Reckon we'd better wire Anson Elms," Potter said, with a contemptuous glance at Lew Barnes.

"Right," agreed Ted Morse, "if I can walk that far. I'm resignin', too, Roberts. I'm for tellin' the company it's impossible to work the mine."

The three crossed the road, ducked under the rails, and headed for the telegraph of-

147

fice. A sideline connected Eagleburg with the railroad far to the south, the settlement's single link with the outside world.

Lew Barnes turned away, to see about getting food and warm drinks for the exhausted miners, who lay strewn or slouched about on the grass. A sudden howl of hatred smashed the air. The men began rising, and a leader shouted:

"There — that's Carlton! He's boss of 'em all, damn him."

"Let's go git him, boys! Lynch him!"

Hastily, Lew Barnes looked toward the Bull's Head. John Carlton and Sam Wills had come outside to see what went on. A furious, red-faced miner fired a revolver at the tall chief of the cowmen. The slug ripped splinters from the board front of the saloon.

The sheriff went hopping across the dusty street.

"Git outa sight, John!" he bellowed.

Face coldly set, John Carlton swept the miners with his strong eyes. Then he shrugged, slowly turned and disappeared inside the Bull's Head. A mob of angry miners came surging over the road. Lew Barnes hopped inside the saloon. He jumped back out a few seconds later with a sawed-off double-barreled shotgun in his hands.

"Stand back," he shouted.

The front men in the mob stopped. Those behind were pushing, and they shoved the foremost on. Barnes fired a scattering charge over their heads, and the heavy blast of the shotgun cooled some of their ardor.

"I'll shoot the first man steps on this porch. Git back across the plaza and stay there. In a jiffy I'll serve yuh coffee and hot food."

The growl of the mob diminished. The idea of a meal subdued their fighting blood. The crisis passed when those in the rear went back, flinging themselves to the grass.

Through the evening and the night, Sheriff Lew Barnes and his deputies had their hands full, patrolling Eagleburg. They had to make sure that the miners, after being fed and rested, did not attempt to charge the quarters where John Carlton and his friends were staying. Fred was to be brought before the justice of the peace in the morning. Carlton insisted on remaining. He wanted to be certain that no out-of-hand miners' mob took his son out of the jail.

The day broke cloudy. A biting wind swept black clouds across a gray sky, bringing with it stinging grit from the dry land west and north of town.

Court was held in the front room of the little lockup. An elderly local judge presided. His heavily armed deputies placed strategically around the building, Lew Barnes brought in witnesses and kept order.

There was grim evidence — half a dozen gold bars stamped with the Pecos Lady mark. Deputies were sworn in and they took the stand. So did Lew Barnes. They described how Fred Carlton had been caught in the line shack where the gold was hidden. They told of the shot he had fired as they came up. After them, Lew Barnes fetched in David Roberts, who pointed an accusing finger at Fred Carlton.

"I've seen that man fire on us. And others present in this courtroom fired on us as well." He glared significantly at John Carlton and Sam Wills.

"Stick to the point, witness," the judge ordered.

Lew Barnes was watching every instant for signs of a flareup. The atmosphere was tense with hatred. He had taken guns from everyone he brought inside. But there were plenty of each side gathered at either end of the town.

Spruced up some, but still showing the effects of what they had gone through, half a dozen miners came in one by one. Each identified Fred Carlton as having fired at them on several occasions.

The hearing ended. The lawyers finished their speeches. The witnesses had all been heard. Now the judge frowned over his glasses.

"Hafta hold yuh, Carlton — for murder. In yore charge, Sheriff Barnes. Trial'll start week from Monday."

Stunned, Fred Carlton walked blindly back into the little cell.

"I can't stand it," he muttered.

John Carlton's face was an inexpressive mask hiding the pain that was in his heart. He stalked from the court, followed by his friends. As he appeared outside, an angry murmur of hate came from groups of miners. Carlton did not deign to look at them. He walked slowly across the plaza.

Charlie Heidt rolled up, met his boss on the veranda of the Cowboys' Rest.

"What yuh say, Boss? Want us to take him outa there?"

"No. Git outa town, Heidt — you and yore hotheads. I'm stayin', but the Law will be upheld."

Heidt shrugged, swung on his spurred high-boots. He hit the back of his mustang without touching the ground, and spurred off west into the chaparral.

The hours dragged like eons for Fred Carlton. The cell was dark. Wind whistled about the brick corners, pelting the thick adobe walls with small pebbles and gritty dust. Elsie came to see him in the late afternoon, bringing hot food. He cheered up at sight of his sweetheart.

"They're selling the Pecos Lady, I hear," the girl told him. "David Roberts has been given the power to sell it by the owners in Austin. There's an agent in town, some lawyer who's taking the mine."

"They'll never git to work it," Fred declared. "Damn their lyin' hearts and souls!"

He was bitter. He knew he was innocent, yet the miners were determined he go to prison. Along with most of the other cowmen of the district, he had exchanged shots with the miners. But always it had been on extreme provocation and in hot blood, man to man. He had not helped in the awful massacres nor stolen any gold.

Elsie stayed with him till after dark. The wind increased, blowing madly over the town, shrieking in the mesquite. Eagleburg brooded, tense and dangerous. John Carlton held back the infuriated cowmen who believed that Fred was being framed. Only the power of the tall chief of the Bar C kept the hot-blooded cowboys directly in hand.

About 9 o'clock Elsie left to join her father, after kissing Fred good night. Fred lay down on the hard bunk and stared at the pale rectangle of the smashed window. It seemed hours before sleep brought relief from anxiety and boredom. He felt his courage would seep away if he must endure it long.

He woke abruptly. Burning unevenly in the draught a candle moved across the outer room toward his cell. Fred sat up.

"Who the hell's that?" he demanded.

"It's me." He recognized Shorty, one of Sheriff Barnes' deputies.

"What's wrong?" Fred asked anxiously.

Shorty paused in embarrassment. He didn't know how to put it.

"They've jest drygulched yore father."

Chapter XIV
Runaway!

Like a shadow in the shadows, Jim Hatfield slipped toward the lighted windows of the A Bar O ranch house. He hoped to find his quarry there — Al Osman, chief of gunmen for the syndicate that coveted the Reeves County range. Through his swift and clever work, the Ranger had traced many crimes to Osman. He had a number of unfinished riddles whose answer he was sure Osman could furnish. A judge of men under stress, Hatfield guessed that the sneering syndicate boss was afraid of him. He now meant to make good use of that emotion.

Perhaps because of his punctured hand, Osman had not led the pack of gunmen devils. Mounted on Bar C, Straight A, and other brands of the neighboring range, masked and fixed up like Carlton's cowmen, they had attacked the retreating miners from the Pecos Lady.

The killer horde had run Hatfield for

miles, south along the uneven, ragged foothills of the mountains. He had drawn them on, keeping just out of gunshot. But he had slowed a bit now and then to fool them or pick off an over-eager leader. For two hours they had chased him, before they realized that nothing on legs could overtake that fleet-footed golden flash the Ranger rode.

When their mounts were lathered and breathing hard, they had quit.

His ruse had drawn them off the miners — at least until they could pass through the worst of the badlands. After that they could fight off the gunnies in the open. The horde shook guns and fists at the cool Ranger. He stopped with them and turned, watching them as they began to ride back northeast.

Probably they had instructions to harass the miners. They must have feared their prey would escape altogether.

The Ranger had given the Pecos Lady men a start. Now his vital business was at the A Bar O. Therefore he rode west, and crossed the mountain shoulder toward the syndicate spread. Night had hardly fallen when he approached the big house.

A peek through a window showed several wounded gunnies lying about. Their injuries had been bandaged up. But Osman was not in sight.

"Now where did snaky rascal go to?" Hatfield mused.

He drew back as hoofs clopped hollowly on the bridge across Sargent Creek. A rider flashed to a sliding stop at the front of the house, and threw himself from his sweated saddle.

It was Kansas Phil. The desperado was covered with dust. He jerked down the bandanna mask over his hard features as he jumped up on the veranda.

"He's in an all-fired hurry," thought Hatfield, watching and listening intently.

"Say, where's Osman?" demanded Phil breathlessly.

A man whose leg was roughly splinted, replied. "Went out an hour ago, Phil. What's wrong?"

"Nuthin' at all," Kansas Phil replied.

But the squat, swarthy Phil pivoted on his spurs. He passed within six feet of Hatfield, who crouched motionless in the black shadows at the end of the ranch house. So engrossed was Kansas Phil in his own thoughts that he never looked around. He hurried across the yard, rounded a corral fence, and disappeared inside a small shack.

Hatfield reckoned he was hunting Al Osman, so he followed soundlessly, a flitting wraith in the spotty light. Phil was inside the hut. The door, which had had a padlock on it, was open. Hatfield looked through the crack.

Phil was bent over. He pulled out some boards and stones that had covered a hole in the earthen floor of the shack.

"Empty!" Hatfield heard him growl. The squat man straightened up, cursing, raving a blue streak. "Damn his dirty heart and soul, I knowed he'd done it!"

The Ranger watched. Enraged, Kansas Phil checked his six-guns, made sure they were fully loaded. Hatfield was back out of sight when Phil blew out the candle stub he had lit, and came charging full speed from the hut.

Phil actually ran, chaps rustling on stubby bow legs, toward his horse.

"Reckon he'll find Osman if anybody kin," Hatfield thought. "I'll stay with him."

The mustang Kansas Phil had ridden in was spent. Blood oozed from spots where the gunny had spurred him. Some hunch that Hatfield did not yet understand had brought Phil hunting for Al Osman.

Phil grabbed the animal's reins, jerked the mustang's head around, and began to unsaddle. He crossed toward a corral in which were the dark shapes of fresh horses. Hatfield slipped into the hut. He shaded a match in the palm of one big hand, and stared into the big cache hole in the hut floor. There was a bunk along the side. Perhaps Osman had slept here, guarding whatever had been in the now empty cavity.

On his knees, the Ranger peered in the good-sized hole. Something gleamed back from the little flare of match light. He reached in, picked a tiny flake of golden substance from the sharp stone that stuck out a foot from the top.

His eyes widened, then a puzzled frown came across his forehead. He felt the flake between his fingers. The match burned his thumb, and he dropped it.

"Huh," he muttered, shaking his head.

He looked from the door, saw that Kansas Phil had finished saddling up a fresh mustang. Not wanting to lose sight of the desperado, he hurried back. The sorrel came to him, muzzled his hand.

Kansas Phil hit the narrow trail leading westward into the wilderness. There were more mountains that way. But finally, through passes to the south, the Rio Grande and Mexico could be reached.

Every fibre of the tall Ranger was alert, ready for instantaneous action. He rode the winding, dangerous trail after Kansas Phil, the squat drygulching lieutenant of the criminal syndicate that was trying to gain control of the range. From the way Phil acted tonight, and from what he had observed back at the A Bar O, the Ranger concluded that Kansas Phil suspected his boss of a doublecross.

Behind the rugged mountains in which the Pecos Lady mine was situated, the hills dropped in undulating waves, broken by razor-back ridges and rock aisles. There was rangeland here. Cattle roamed the *barrancos,* hunting for grama grass and other nutritious fodder of the region.

Inky shadows of high mesquite cut the trail. In sandy flats were the candelabra of giant cacti, or an *ocotillo* with its high, graceful flower wand. Coming from the west into Hatfield's face as he rode the wind carried an aromatic scent from the sagebrush and creosote bushes. Here and there ratama followed some line of rocks. Overhead the sky was clear, the moon coming up.

"He's shore beatin' the leather, Goldy," murmured the Ranger.

His nostrils were widened, sniffing at the breeze. A faint dust haze hung in the air, picked up by the beating hoofs of Phil's swift gray mustang. The officer was using this sense to follow his man. A good tracker must use sight, hearing, touch, taste, and smell and a mysterious sixth sense. Blue-steel six-guns were ready in their pliant holsters. The rifle was snugged in the saddle-boot, for any challenge from the quarry ahead must be met in the flash of an eye.

Mile after mile rolled up and under the swift sorrel's flying hoofs. But now the way was rising steeply, and westward loomed great black mountains. The Ranger stopped the golden gelding. He sat perfectly motion-less, listening. And the wind in his face brought no sound of the horseman ahead, no freshly risen alkali dust. . . .

"Turned off. We missed it," he muttered, swinging the horse.

He hunted back. Several hundred yards east, by careful observation, he located the gap in the mesquite wall. He knelt, ran a hand over the dark ground that was shad-owed by the bush. His sensitive fingers felt the fresh depressions.

"Huh! Bunch of hosses," he told Goldy, remounting and starting south through the dry valley.

The wind now carried the dust away from his trail, and sound as well. But he was sure he was on the right track. An hour's run south, across rocky shale underfooting, and the sorrel sniffed a warning.

Hatfield instantly stopped, dismounted, and left the sorrel. Soundlessly he hurried forward on foot. He rounded a turn in the trail through thorny chaparral. First his nostrils caught the scent of wood smoke sharpening the air. Then he saw the dark shapes of a dozen horses standing in a tiny clearing.

A small fire still burned, the coals reddening in the puffs of wind. A blanket had been spread out for a bed, and a coffee pot and frying pan were close by.

The two men stood illuminated by the moonlight and the faint ruby glow cast by the dying fire. Hatfield easily recognized them as Al Osman and Kansas Phil.

Inching in, the Ranger could make out Osman's face, a pale oval in the eerie light. The squat Phil had his wide back to Hatfield and was engaged in telling Osman what he thought of him.

"Yuh dirty, doublecrossin' rat," Kansas Phil swore, his six-gun glinting as he kept Osman pinned at a distance of ten feet. "I savvied what yuh was up to! Soon as I could, I slipped away from the boys and rode back. Yuh couldn't ride, yore hand hurt too much!" Phil was sneering at Osman in triumph, gloating over his own sharp wits at having out-maneuvered his boss.

"Aw, cut it out, Phil," soothed Osman.

But he was nervous under the gun, and his hands made two lighter patches at his shoulders as he kept them up. Phil had come up on him as he slept. Osman had thought he had a long enough start for a rest.

"Packed it all and run for Chihuahua! Why, if I was a fool like the others, I'd be over at Eagleburg now, 'stead of right here holdin' a royal flush. I allus knowed yuh was yeller. Yuh'd soon as not stab yore own mother in the back for money."

"Quit it," Osman said again, nervously. "Why don't yuh come along, Phil? I'd've told yuh if I could. C'mon, holster yore gun and we'll split fifty-fifty."

"Fifty-fifty! That's a good 'un," hooted Phil. His voice turned suddenly cruel, gratingly harsh. "Buzzard-bait, that's what yuh are now, Osman."

Hatfield's muscles grew ready. He knew Phil meant to kill Al Osman in a moment. Osman knew it too. He began begging for mercy in a hysterical, high-pitched voice. Both men were so engrossed in their own conflict that they had no suspicion of the

Ranger's presence.

"No, no, Phil — don't shoot!" panted Osman. "We been pals, me'n you. I got leery of that big Ranger jigger, I tell yuh. He's hot on our trail — would've got us in the end. Look how he fooled us after I figured I'd drygulched him in Eagleburg that night! He had us at the Pecos Lady, on'y the cowmen come along and give us a chance to run for it. It was him plugged my hand. He was right outside the ranch house, spyin' on us. He saved Heidt's bunch. I hadda git clear of him. He's a devil —"

"Dry up, yuh coyote! The Chief'll kill that sneakin' Ranger. What kin one man do against an army? I bet he's snoozin' in the bush fifty miles from here right now."

"The Chief's tough," Osman said slowly. "But that Ranger's tougher, I tell yuh. I've heard of Hatfield afore. He kilt a pal of mine on the Border last year — swept up his whole gang. Healthiest place is where that Ranger ain't."

"Huh. Yuh shore got a skunk streak up yore spine," growled Kansas Phil. "Me, I suspicioned yuh all along. I'm s'prised the Chief trusted yuh with all that stuff."

"Half of it's yores," said Osman eagerly, hope in his voice. "Lemme put down my arms, Phil. They're gittin' tired —"

163

"I'll fix that," Phil declared grimly. He dug his boots into the sandy dirt and spread them wide. He leaned forward a bit.

Osman gave a strangled, frightened bleat. "Don't — don't —"

"I'm takin' both ends of that fifty-fifty split," gritted Phil, lashing himself to killing pitch. "I'll have that spree in Monterey alone!"

The clear, incisive voice of the Ranger, distinct as a pistol shot, cut the aromatic night air.

"Drop yore gun, Kansas Phil. Yuh're under arrest."

Chapter XV
Showdown

Jim Hatfield's command halted the two gunny chiefs as though they had suddenly been hit by paralysis. Both of them tensed. His six-shooter black against the firelight, Phil froze as he was. The muzzle of his Colt still pointed at Al Osman, who still kept up his hands.

For the moment they did not place him exactly. But both of them were aware that they were covered.

Then Phil gasped. Explosively his breath shot from his lungs. A moment later he asked tentatively:

"Who — where are yuh?"

"Drop the gun, I said."

Kansas Phil let the pistol fall to the earth. He raised his hands.

Jim Hatfield rose up from his crouch and stepped into the circle of light.

"It's him — I knowed it!" cried Osman. His dark eyes glowed with new fear. "I told

165

yuh so, yuh fool!"

Slowly, so his movement would not be misconstrued, the squat desperado turned his head. His bearded face worked nervously and he blinked as he took in the tall Ranger stepping toward them. Hatfield's slim hands swung easily at his narrow hips, where the blue-steel six-guns still reposed in their supple holsters.

"I ain't had much chance to snooze lately," he drawled mildly, "thanks to you boys."

The mildness fooled Phil, as it had fooled others of his ilk in the past. He was more impetuous than Osman, but without the evil cunning of the sneering A Bar O boss. Kansas Phil believed in action. Hatfield had no gun out. Kansas Phil had a second weapon in his left-hand holster.

He went for it. His hand streaked from his shoulder. Unerringly he gripped the walnut stock. The steel cleared, gleamed in the light. The draw was too fast to follow with the eye. Kansas Phil handled his gun as many fighters did. The weapon cocked by its own weight, thumb on hammer, as it flashed out.

Jim Hatfield was ready for the play. He did not miss the shifting of Phil's hand as it started.

With blinding speed the blue-steel Colt

cleared leather and roared. A red-yellow flash lighted the cold, grim face of the tall Ranger.

He felt Phil's slug tear through a flap of his chaps. But the squat desperado flipped back, gun flying into the bushes, arms out as he handed in his checks.

Hatfield's slug had drilled through his teeth and into the brain. Kansas Phil died, gurgling through the gush of blood that was choking him.

Al Osman had no guns on. Kansas Phil had seen to that before nudging him awake with his pistol. But the lean boss of the A Bar O was desperately afraid of Jim Hatfield. When the Ranger went into action against Kansas Phil, he had been forced to use every ounce of concentration. Instantly Osman fell flat on his belly and crawled into the bushes.

Hatfield whirled to put a slug near him, to scare him into surrender. But Osman's fright went beyond that. His one idea was to escape from the unerring brain that had unraveled the syndicate's plot against the range.

"C'mere, Osman," roared the Ranger, jumping after him. He did not wish to kill the lean gunny. He considered Al Osman important enough for capture alive.

He heard Osman running through the chaparral. The A Bar O boss had doubled back past the clearing as the Ranger started south into the bush. Hatfield changed his direction. He bounded across the clearing and back along the winding trail.

A moment later he glimpsed the dark figure of his quarry. Osman burst from the chaparral and hit Goldy's saddle in a running frog-leap.

Osman dug the spurs in and beat the sorrel with his fist, urging him on. The gelding obeyed, flashing north, away from his master. Nothing that Osman had left behind could overtake the Ranger's pet.

"Goldy! Goldy! C'mere, boy," shouted Hatfield, running up the trail. He whistled shrill blasts.

The trained sorrel slowed. Osman gored him, beat him on for a few yards. But Hatfield's clear voice reached the sorrel.

"Buck, Goldy, buck!"

Obediently the animal began to buck. He cleared the ground with all four feet, head down despite the sharp bit that Osman jerked into his tender lips. Legs stiff, the golden gelding bounced up and down, turning and twisting in the air.

Hatfield was running full-tilt toward them. Osman was an expert rider and could not be unseated. He cursed the recalcitrant sorrel, tried to force him on. Then, as his teeth rattled in his head, he saw Hatfield bounding at him.

In a panic of terror, he snatched at the rifle in its boot. He held the leather with his steely legs, which had been born to the saddle. The Winchester came out and up. Osman turned to take the best aim he could.

The Ranger swerved aside into the bushes. He could not shoot and chance hitting the moving horse. Nor did he want to kill Al Osman. A bullet from the rifle spat through the leaves. But aim was too difficult with the madly gyrating horse underneath him.

"Here, Goldy! This way —"

The gelding sought to respond. He bounced up and down with crow-hops that jarred Osman's teeth and brought water into the hombre's narrowed eyes.

Suddenly the big sorrel reared high on his hind legs. For an instant Hatfield thought he meant to fall back, crush Osman under his weight. . . .

With a curse, Hatfield leaped out on the trail. He grasped the bridle, brought Goldy's head down. Osman was swinging the rifle around, but it was a clumsy weapon at such close range.

Hatfield's hand flashed up, caught the gun. He ripped it from Osman's hold. Close against the lathered, heaving ribs of the horse, the Ranger grasped Osman's wrist and jerked with all his weight. The thin devil lurched from his seat.

Osman fell under him. Hatfield paused. The sorrel quit bucking and stood quivering. His eyes were red, for blood flowed down his flanks from the spur gouges.

Osman was beyond reason. In a mad, hysterical panic, his arms flailed the Ranger, catching him several sharp blows in the face. He kicked with spurred boots at the big hombre. He was certain Hatfield meant to kill him.

The Ranger lost his patience, for Osman refused to heed his commands. Hatfield broke down the man's guard by main strength, grasped him by the shirt and jerked him to his feet. He drove a jolting punch to Osman's mouth that crushed the lips against the teeth. Only the fact that Hatfield held him kept Osman from falling head over heels. The Ranger hit him again.

"And this is for usin' yore spurs on my hoss!"

The pain brought Osman to some vestige of sanity. He collapsed, held up limply by Hatfield. Whimpering, his breath came in terrible sobs through the blood that spurted from his cut lips.

"Damn yuh! So it was you who drygulched me in Eagleburg!" snarled the Ranger.

One hand sufficed to hold up his prisoner. The steely eyes of the officer drilled straight to Osman's soul. It was his intention to frighten Osman so the lean gunny chief would talk, tell all he knew. With such murderous killers Jim Hatfield could show a feral ferocity that far outdid any efforts on their parts. Mild as the Ranger behaved with decent folk, against men like Osman he was tougher than the worst of outlaws. It was the only way with many of them.

A punch or two more, a kick back toward the little clearing, and Osman was completely subdued. Realizing that Hatfield did not mean to kill him instantly, Osman tried to regain some of his sneering poise.

"This here's a showdown, Osman," growled Hatfield.

He threw the A Bar O boss to the dirt and towered over him.

"What yuh mean?" snapped Osman, breath still fast. He watched the Ranger

171

every second.

"There's some things I want to know," Hatfield said. "And yuh're goin' to tell me. First, who's yore chief in this game?"

"Why should I talk?"

"Because," Hatfield replied, "otherwise I'll take yore hide right off yore bones. I reckon I don't need to tell yuh who and what I am. From yore talk with Phil here" — the Ranger spurned the dead body with a boot toe — "yuh know."

"Why should I talk?" repeated Osman. "Yuh got me."

His eyes glanced quickly past Hatfield, at the picketed horses on the other side of the trail. As swiftly, Osman looked back at the Ranger.

Silently Hatfield turned and crossed to the nearest horse. It carried a compact load, small packs that balanced each other on either side. Hatfield felt the canvas covered bags, touched a cool, metallic surface.

From the corner of his eye, Hatfield watched the beaten Osman. He led the pack-horse back to the fire and threw on some of the dry brush Osman had collected nearby. Then he drew his sheath knife and cut the canvas and bag. A golden ingot, a foot long, thudded to the ground. Another clanked on top of it.

Osman's eyes glowed with frustrated greed. Regret clawed at his soul. Here was a fortune he might have had!

"I was wonderin'," drawled the Ranger, his veiled eyes regarding the thin, sneer-lipped man, "how much yuh keer 'bout this chief of yores. Mebbe yuh figgered on git-tin' help from him later, huh? You s'pose he really trusted yuh with all that gold you and yore pals raided from the Pecos Lady?"

Osman started, scowled. The Ranger went on softly:

"Yuh stole range hosses and masked yore men. They was mistaken, as yuh intended, for local cowmen. Yuh massacred them miner trains, run the gold to the A Bar O and buried it in that shack yuh slept in."

The exact knowledge the Ranger pos-sessed shook Al Osman.

"Yuh — yuh're a devil!" the frightened Osman hissed.

"However, couple of things, 'sides won-derin' why this chief of yores would trust yuh, puzzled me, Osman. I found a queer flake of somethin' stuck to a sharp rock in yore cache hole back at the hut. And did yuh hear that clank jest now?"

With his sheath knife, Hatfield dug hard at the yellow bar, a rough ingot of gold. But his knife scratched across the surface. Flakes followed in its track. He kept scraping. Presently, under the yellow layer, he exposed a metal with a dull, silvery surface.

"That's steel, covered with a thick layer of gold paint," drawled the Ranger. "I reckon yore chief didn't trust yuh any too far, Osman!"

Al Osman leaped to his feet, cursing a blue streak. He picked up the fake ingot, stared at it until his dark eyes bulged.

"Why, the dirty, doublecrossin' sidewinder!" he shrieked. "I — I risked my neck for that worthless stuff!" Pride cut, knowing he had been made a fool of, Al Osman hit bottom. "Damn him. No wonder he wanted all them fellers kilt! All the time he had the stuff for himself —"

"How about it?" broke in Jim Hatfield. "Yuh oughta be convinced now, Osman. We're headin' for Eagleburg."

"Them ranchers'll string me up if they git me," Osman moaned, wiping the sweat from his bruised, bleeding face.

"Not with me around, they won't. Yuh got a chance to live, if you obey me."

Al Osman hesitated. He stared up into the long, grim face of the Ranger.

"Okay. Let's git goin'. We kin talk as we ride."

Hatfield cut off the worthless packs and turned the horses loose. Osman had a fast animal picketed nearby. The Ranger rubbed down his sorrel, tightened his loosened cinches, and swung into the leather.

Ahead, as they turned eastward, lay Eagle-burg and the minions of Al Osman's chief.

Chapter XVI
Ride Against Death

From Al Osman's confession, gleaned sentence by sentence as they headed eastward, Jim Hatfield knew he dared not pause. Sleep was out of the question. The horses had to have water, and so did the men.

Inexorably the Ranger pushed on for Eagleburg. Osman informed him that after harassing the miners in their retreat from the Pecos Lady, the gunnies had orders to stand by outside the town and be ready for duty in case the Chief needed them. There was to be a final extermination of ranchers and miners.

"He wanted the mine and he needed a lot of the range, too," Osman explained. "That's where we come in. The syndicate was to suck in the big ranches as we busted 'em."

John Carlton was not at the Bar C. Hatfield crossed the Sargent bridge. There he was informed that the leader of the cowmen had ridden to Eagleburg.

"All gone, boys too," the Chinese cook grinned happily.

The day had broken cloudy, the wind veering and scudding the dark shapes before it across the lowering sky. Gritty dust spattered the riders until they had to keep their bandannas up across mouth and nose. Their heads were down to the gusts that whirled about them, rattling the dry pods of the mesquite.

It was night when they saw below them the yellow, twinkling lights of Eagleburg. The bush was so black that the spent horses had to sense the way.

Suddenly men faced them, riders who spurred from the sides of the main road to town. Hatfield heard the sharp challenge given, guessed their identity. He had expected to run into gunmen patrols near the town. But nothing could turn him aside. The need for haste was too great.

Osman's hands were tied with rawhide, fastened by a yard length to his saddle horn. The Ranger's lariat was taut behind the sorrel, for he was towing his prisoner.

The tall Ranger's six-gun roared. Flame stabbed at the killers who sought to block them. A man crashed dead from his saddle.

Another shrieked as lead drilled his shoulder. Spurs lightly touching, Hatfield drove the sorrel at them, firing as he came.

They melted from the path like sugar before a rushing river. Shots answered his, but they merely tore by. He swung, shooting past Osman, emptying a Colt at the spot where they had tried to stop him. The flares of the guns were blinding in the blackness of the night.

Suddenly they were through. The Ranger was scarcely aware of the torn flesh where a blind bullet had ripped his left forearm.

Osman was swearing. He had felt that the singing lead from his erstwhile mates came too close for comfort.

"We're through," Hatfield shouted, and spurred on.

With a last dash that took them out of the chaparral to the outskirts of the settlement, Jim Hatfield headed for the plaza.

Riding across the open space, he heard approaching gunshots and the howling of furious men. The sorrel checked, hung his head. His heaving ribs were sticky with dust and sweat. Osman's animal was shaking, leg splaying out in weariness.

From the west side of the plaza Hatfield saw young Charlie Heidt, cutting from the houses. Heidt was whooping it up at the head of a packed mass of cowmen who clutched their guns viciously.

A rifle blasted from the other end. The Pecos Lady miners stood there, waiting for the final battle to begin.

The Ranger lowered his bandanna, swung Goldy to face the approaching cowmen.

"Heidt!" he roared.

The hot-blooded waddy heard his stentorian shout, jerked back on his reins. His mustang rearing and dancing, he came toward Hatfield.

"Who the hell? Why, howdy, Ranger! Yuh're jest in time for the fight. If yuh don't like it, move aside."

Faces hot with fighting blood, his men were pressing behind him. Hatfield had expected to see the younger fellows. But now, since the shooting of John Carlton, older and more level-headed ranchers rode with them.

"Stand back and call yore men off, Heidt."

"Like hell, Ranger. They drygulched Carlton and they got Fred held in the jail, framed for murder. This is the showdown!"

"It is the showdown," drawled Hatfield, so close to the hot-blooded youth that their horses were almost touching. "Call yore men to stop."

Heidt grinned, the tight Stetson strap accentuating the bulldog line of his fighting jaw.

"Okay, boys — *Let's git 'em!*"

A roar of approval went up. Hatfield reached out, grasped the waddy's reins, jerked his horse around.

"Leggo that," snarled Heidt. "I'll —"

The Ranger let go, but only to sweep Heidt from his saddle with a steel arm. Furious, the waddy picked himself up from the dust. His hand dropped to the six-shooter at his hip.

Hatfield sat the sorrel, staring down at him. Heidt stopped his draw, shrugged.

"Well," he growled, "make yore talk, Ranger. But make it quick."

A mutter of anger had risen from Heidt's followers when they saw the tall Ranger knock the youth from his horse. But they knew who Hatfield was, and they followed Heidt's lead.

"Hey — Ranger!" That was Lew Barnes, calling to him from the little lockup where he was treed with his deputies.

The tall sheriff leaped out, waving to Hatfield.

Now the ranchers recognized Al Osman, Hatfield's prisoner, nervously sitting his horse behind the Ranger.

"Say, that's Osman from the A Bar O, the dirty rustler!" cried Heidt. "Gimme a rope!"

"Keep yore trap shut," Hatfield ordered coldly. "This ain't a lynchin' bee I'm gittin' up. Range yore men in line and see there's no shootin'. I hold yuh responsible."

He swung to the sheriff, who came hurrying toward him.

The night wind shrieked through the live oaks of the plaza, swirling dust about them. It confused the brain and blinded the eyes, carrying voices on its forceful bosom. Hatfield tossed the reins of Al Osman's horse to Lew Barnes.

"Keep this pris'ner, Sheriff."

Lights from saloons and homes, from flickering oil lanterns creaking on posts, gave weird illumination to the scene. The muttering of so many voices added to the difficulty of controlling the two antagonistic gangs. From the east end the miners fired several wild shots. Bullets tore over the massed ranchers.

Hatfield leaned down, lips close to Heidt's ear.

"Git yore men inside the Bull's Head. Pronto now! Place 'em in back and keep 'em quiet."

His steely eyes met the hot orbs of the young waddy. For an instant the two strong natures clashed. Then Charlie Heidt replied: "Okay, Ranger."

Alone, Jim Hatfield spurred east toward the miners. They watched him coming, angry faces set, rifles and pistols, clubs gripped and ready for the fray. A slug whipped past his ear. He saw the gun flash, but rode coolly on. Presently he was close on the Pecos Lady men, hunting for their leaders with his quick glance. In the center of the bunch he saw David Roberts. Hatfield walked the golden sorrel toward him.

"Roberts," he called, his voice carrying sharp over the wind. "Calm down yore men and git 'em into the Bull's Head. I got important news for yuh."

"Why should we listen to you?" demanded Roberts angrily. "You're a cowman, deputy."

Then they saw the Ranger badge, which was held before them in a slim, strong hand. They quieted, watching the stern face, set in rigid lines between the black Stetson straps.

"The boss of yore company, Anson Elms, asked the Texas Rangers for help. And I'm it. Yuh've been fooled, and fooled hard, boys. Now Al Osman's goin' to tell yuh the truth."

The miners had seen this hombre in action. They felt his power, the magnetism that the Ranger emanated. The fire died down in their eyes. David Roberts appeared confused, but he finally nodded.

"We're sellin' the Pecos Lady, Ranger. Tonight we're only defending ourselves. The cowmen blame us for the shooting of John Carlton, which we didn't do —"

Shouts came on the wind from up the plaza. To the west, against the dark mass of chaparral, the flashes of guns dotted the bushes. Jim Hatfield turned the magnificent golden sorrel. He rode at full-tilt along the line, pouring six-gun bullets into the mesquite. Answering ones whirled about him, missing as his speed picked up.

He swerved, knowing he must quickly pour the oil of truth on the troubled waters of Eagleburg. The cowmen were turning, angered by the pot-shotting from the chaparral.

"Inside, boys," roared Hatfield, shooing them over to the Bull's Head. Many had already dismounted, and were entering the place. "We'll take care of 'em later."

Sheriff Lew Barnes and his deputies were leading Al Osman to the saloon. Osman staggered along, and took away his hand he had held to his face. It came away bloody. A bullet, sent at long range out of the chaparral, had come close to getting him.

"Hustle him outa danger, Barnes," the Ranger commanded.

He glimpsed young Fred Carlton with the deputies. Sam Wills and his daughter stood on the wooden walk, watching as the Ranger herded miners and cowmen inside the Bull's Head. Fred stared curiously at the tall commanding Ranger. Evidently someone had told him who Hatfield was, for new hope transformed his face.

The gray-green eyes, cold with the darkness of an Arctic sea, swept Eagleburg. The Ranger rode close to David Roberts.

"Where're Potter and Morse?" he asked.

"They were around a little while ago," Roberts replied.

The swinging oil lamps cast their golden glow over the angry faces of both factions. Crowded into the Bull's Head were a couple of hundred miners and cowmen. The Ranger left the sorrel outside, ducked under the hitch-rail. He stalked up on the crowded porch, shoving a way through to the center of the bar. There Lew Barnes stood, with a circle of deputies around Al Osman.

No sneer distorted the lean A Bar O boss' face now. He was thoroughly frightened, for the waddies glared at him with vengeful rage. His eyes sought the serene face of Hatfield, to whom he now looked for protection.

Lew Barnes shook with nervousness as he gripped the Ranger's arm.

"Make it quick and make it good, Ranger!" he whispered. "If'n they explode in here, it'll be hell!"

Hatfield towered over most men, even the big Texans. He raised an arm for silence, began speaking in his deep, drawling, but terrifically effective voice.

"Gents, both cowmen and miners, yuh've been fooled bad, and fooled cruel in these parts. Yuh're fightin' each other instead of the real enemy, who's after the Pecos Lady mine and the range that goes with it. Al Osman, chief of the so-called A Bar O Syndicate, which has rustled local cattle hereabouts, will tell yuh just how it was done."

He seized a chair. Osman, face yellowish under his tan, stood upon it. The lean hombre gulped, glanced again for reassurance at the tall Ranger.

"Go to it, Osman," ordered Hatfield. "Tell 'em what yuh told me!"

Curious, their anger put aside for the moment as they listened, both factions watched the nervous Osman. Abruptly he blurted forth the truth.

"The Ranger's right when he says yuh

were fooled. It was done a-purpose, to smash the mine and the ranchers too. Far as the syndicate goes, why, that was set up so's we could devil the cowmen and finally take over their spreads. Also, it give us a depot for the fightin' men we needed. The main idea, though, was to git the Pecos Lady mine and its gold. There's plenty of it up there in the mountains, and a lot was took out. But we — we —"

He paused and licked his lips, looking at Hatfield with a scared glare in his dark eyes.

"Yuh're safe, Osman," Hatfield drawled. "I guarantee it."

"Well, we acted on order from the Chief, who planned the whole shebang. We fixed ourselves up like local waddies and stole hosses with ranch brands on to ride. Then we raided them gold trains. Sure, we had exact information 'bout 'em. Orders was to — to kill ev'rybody and leave no witnesses. But we was to shoot a ranch hoss or two so's it'd be shore the cowmen'd done the jobs."

Angry rumbles came from the throats of hard hombres. They realized that they had been egged on by a slimy, hidden foe to fight each other to the death.

"There was all sorts of tricks we fixed up,"

went on Osman, nudged by the Ranger. "But we always put blame on one side or the other — made it look like the miners was rustlin' and pot-shottin' at line riders. That was easy. Our Chief knowed that the Austin company couldn't hold out forever, if local folks was dead set against the Pecos Lady. They'd go bust or hafta sell out for a song."

"Why, this is horrible!" exploded David Roberts. "I — I nearly killed them all, with that powder mine! I —"

"Take it easy," soothed Jim Hatfield. "You were heated up to it, Roberts, jest like the others."

"But — but it's certain Fred Carlton was in on those raids on the gold trains," cried Roberts. "He was caught red-handed!"

"That was another of the Chief's cute little tricks," Hatfield insisted. "Osman'll tell yuh."

"Shore, the Chief had it in for John Carlton. 'Sides, Carlton was leader of the cowmen and hadda be busted. The Chief figgered on plantin' the massacres on Fred. I 'ranged that little job myself. We led Carlton over there, put him in the hut — The Chief gimme some gold bars to bury there."

Fred Carlton's face suddenly cleared. The terrible anxiety he had been under for so long slewed off quickly. Smiling, Elsie Wills touched his arm and the two young people stood close together, happy in their love.

"Who's this Chief you speak of, Osman?" demanded David Roberts.

"Look around," drawled Hatfield. "See who's missin', Roberts. *George Potter and Ted Morse!*"

CHAPTER XVII
CHAPARRAL BATTLE

Incredulously, David Roberts and his bearded, battered miners stared at the tall Ranger.

"Why, I can't believe that!" Roberts exclaimed. "Morse, our manager — Potter, sent out here as trouble man —"

"He made trouble, all right," Hatfield remarked dryly. "Morse done what Potter told him to. Potter's chief of the whole dirty shebang. He's out there in the chaparral now, with Osman's gunnies. When he seen me come to town with Osman in tow, he knowed the game was up. There's nuthin' left for him but to ride for it with what he's got."

"He's got plenty," Al Osman rumbled angrily. "All the gold from the Pecos Lady! He fooled me plenty, gents. He used some iron bars painted to look like ingots, damn him."

Jim Hatfield had smashed the terrible tension between the two factions. Cowmen and miners, realizing what had been done to them, stared at each other, enmity wilting under the clear light of the truth.

"You were heated to killin' rage," remarked Hatfield. "The cowmen done battled yuh, miners. But remember that you was shootin' too, and plenty. You were all blinded by Potter's tricks. Bygones're bygones. Osman has told yuh the true way it's been. He's my pris'ner and I'm holdin' him safe."

Any idea of lynching Al Osman, the boss of the so-called syndicate, was given up. Men's eyes fell before the level gaze of the Ranger's gray-green gaze. He would protect his captive against any attempts that wild riders might think up, and they knew it.

Miners and waddies began fraternizing. Drinks were called for. Voices rose throughout the Bull's Head as the exciting events were discussed and puzzling actions cleared.

But Jim Hatfield could not rest. There remained too much to be done, although he had prevented the final battle that would have decimated both sides. Young Fred Carlton pushed up to him, a friendly grin on his handsome face, his hand stuck out.

"I want to shake yore hand," Fred cried. "Thanks for savin' me from hell, Ranger

Hatfield. Tonight's the first time I've seen yuh, but —"

"I sorta had a peek at yuh, Fred," Hatfield told him kindly, taking his hand. He explained how he had observed the young fellow in the wilds, when Lew Barnes had led him past the Ranger's hideout. "Yuh didn't look like a killer to me, so I checked up on yore story. That give me a lead to the A Bar O. Come on outside, will yuh?"

Obediently Fred Carlton trailed the tall Ranger out of the saloon. His glance was admiring as he took in Hatfield's supple, powerful figure. The narrow hips and wide shoulders of Texas' greatest fighting man hinted at the feline ripple of powerful muscles beneath the torn clothing.

"He's like a tiger, on'y a good one," Fred thought, inspired by the big fellow who alone could snatch him from the horrible situation that had no other possible escape. "Why, I'd foller him to hell and back! I'd shore hate to be an outlaw and tangle with him!"

Hatfield turned, looking into Fred's eyes.

"How bad's yore Dad hurt?" he inquired.

"His leg's smashed, Ranger," replied Fred. "He's sufferin' a lot, but he'll get well in time. He's lyin' over at the Cowboys' Rest. Say, I just got to thank yuh for all yuh've done. I'm so relieved I could dance a jig."

"Save the dance till the shootin' begins," drawled Hatfield. "Take me to yore father. I wanta talk to him."

The two stalwart men strode west along the edge of the plaza. The night wind blasted them with dust and loose leaves from the live oaks. Hatfield glanced over at the back wall of the chaparral. Out there, lurking somewhere in the darkness rode his arch-enemy. George Potter was the one man responsible for the havoc and murder spread over the land. And out there with him Potter had a hundred gunnies, formerly under Al Osman.

"Guess he's took command himself by now," mused the tall Ranger. "I busted through their line 'fore they could concentrate."

Fred led the way into the back room where John Carlton lay on his bed of pain. The giant figure was stretched out flat on a cot, with a chair at the bottom because he was too long for a bed. His deep-set eyes burned, but not so much at the anguish of physical torture. He fought because he had to lie there helpless, unable to move a finger to help. His only son was locked behind prison bars, awaiting trial for murder. Nothing could have tortured the brave John Carl-ton as that did.

His face lighted when he saw Fred, went somber as he recognized the Law. But he shook the tall Ranger's extended hand and muttered:

"I tried to hold 'em to the Law, but they got outa control when I was drygulched."

"That's why it was done, Carlton. Potter wasn't ready yet for yuh to make peace. He wanted both sides crushed. Did yuh glimpse who shot yuh?"

Carlton shook his head. His smashed leg was splinted to the pelvis by a piece of board, tied with heavy bandage to hold the bone ends together.

"I was sittin' in the bar with Wills when a masked hombre stuck a gun through the winder and yelled, 'This is from the Pecos Lady, Carlton!' Sam run out but the feller'd gone. Wills picked up that there gantlet on the table, right outside the winder."

On the table lay a heavy leather glove with fancy-trimmed wristlets. It was the sort necessary in riding the thorny chaparral of the Southwest, where every plant stung, stuck or smelled. The tall Ranger stepped up, looked it over curiously. It was a right-hand glove, scratched by thorns. Evidently the killer had removed the thick leather so he could get his fingers through the trigger guard of his Colt. Feeling it, smelling it, regarding it, Hatfield found a small lump of wool stuffed in the end of one finger.

"Huh," he grunted. "I'll jest take this with me, Carlton. Al Osman may be able to say whose it is."

He had work to do. Quickly he informed John that his son was clear of all charges. The look in the big rancher chief's eyes repaid the Ranger for all his fighting and riding.

Sheriff Barnes had discreetly removed Al Osman to a rear room, where the former boss of the A Bar O Syndicate was held under guard. Jim Hatfield found the slim gunny there, showed him the gantlet.

"Shore, I've seen it. Belongs to Potter," Osman growled. He replied to the Ranger's next question, "No, never knowed Potter till he picked me up on the Border for this job."

Jim Hatfield seldom missed a trick. The glove left behind by Carlton's drygulcher grew in importance as he turned all the events over in his keen, orderly brain. "Huh," he grunted at last, rising and starting out. "Wonder if it could be? Hafta wire Austin!"

He discovered the telegraph operator in the saloon. The hombre agreed to send a message to McDowell at once.

Outside again, he stared sternly at the black chaparral wall about Eagleburg, west and north. The golden sorrel came at his shrill whistling. He mounted and rode for the western road. As he neared the bush, guns blazed at him. Slugs whistled close to his ear, clipped his leather. His six-shooter answered as he pivoted the sorrel, galloping back out of range.

"So's he's left 'em to block me," he grunted, flipping blood from a new scratch in his left hand.

He rode the sorrel back to the Bull's Head. His arrival in the main room was the signal for another rousing cheer. The Ranger raised an arm over his Stetson for silence. Jim Hatfield did not enjoy public ovations — he was too modest a man for that.

"Gents," he drawled, "there's an army of gunnies lined up west of town. They're the real enemies yuh've been honin' to meet!"

Charlie Heidt jumped to the bar.

"What say, boys?" he shouted. "Are we with him?"

A roar of assent went up. Men began checking over their rifles and pistols for the battle. These fighters had been yearning to come to grips with the enemies who had so long hounded them with death. Set on the right track by the Ranger, it was now difficult to restrain them.

"Take it easy," Hatfield commanded, looking over his pick-up army, inspired by the great fighting general who directed them. "Heidt, you got charge of yore waddies. I want yuh to sneak along Sargent Creek on the south and head west. When yuh figger yuh're far enough on, swing north through the bush. Sheriff Barnes, take the miners and git up to the north. Then head west like the cowmen. Turn south, meetin' Heidt."

"Pincers," nodded Lew Barnes. "But what if they fade away from us 'fore we kin close?"

"That's up to me," explained Hatfield. "Both bunches'll leave the saloon by the back. Stay in the dark of the alleys. Yuh'll hafta sift around and find hosses without showin' yoreselves, savvy? In the meantime I want a dozen sharpshooters — How 'bout you deputies?"

Lew Barnes' deputies were willing. All were expert riders and good shots.

Following their leaders, miners and cowmen hurried from the back door of the Bull's Head. There were horses in various stables, and others with reins lying over hitch-racks that were deeply shadowed in the side passages beside the buildings. The two columns were started, while Jim Hatfield openly led his dozen into the street. They mounted. Fronted by the Ranger, they trotted across the plaza in full sight.

"Spread out, boys," commanded Hatfield. "When it starts, fan yore bullets into the chaparral."

As they came within gun range of the black bush wall, slugs began shrieking around them.

"Keep movin' fast! Ride up and down!"

Full-tilt, the masterful riders spurred their mustangs up and down, whooping and shooting into the bush. The beating hoofs ripped up dust, swirled by the wind into a clouding screen over the plaza. By the volume of fire from the bush, Hatfield guessed that the bulk of the gunnies were concentrating on his dozen.

Keeping back, the Ranger occupied them with his strategy. Their hatred for the tall Ranger, who single-handed had so cramped their style, was overwhelming. It kept them where they were until Hatfield figured Heidt and Barnes must be in position.

Fifteen minutes later, in the wild night, the fire from the A Bar O men slackened. In the high mesquite, confused shouts and new shooting came on the wind to the

Ranger's alert ear.

"Take cover, boys. They'll be breakin' out in a minute!" he roared.

Trees and building walls were handy, and there the deputies scattered for concealment. Jim Hatfield stayed close to the bush wall. The shooting in there was terrific now. He could see the flashing of hundreds of guns. Caught by the closing pincers of the two columns of Hatfield's fighters, the hired killers of the A Bar O realized too late what they had permitted the enemy to do. Pressed from three sides, they rode into death at the hands of miners and cowmen.

The awful battle was raging in the chaparral. It was hard to recognize friend from foe in there. Men were locked in fierce combat, exchanging bullet for bullet at a distance of a few feet.

"Be ready when they flush out," Hatfield called to his men. "I'm goin' in!"

He spurred toward the bush wall. A dozen panicked gunnies burst forth, close to the Ranger. His hot Colts blasted into them, driving them right into the ready rifles of the deputies. They began picking off the maddened riders as they sought a way of escape along the lighted plaza.

Goldy hit the chaparral. A sharp *pop* sounded as the beautiful sorrel twisted sideward to break away. Thorns tore at the horse's hide and the thick leather of the tall Ranger, who rode with guns alert. A few stragglers were filtering through, one or two at a time. But the main gang of gunmen still fought out there. Flares of pistols lit the dark bush a few hundred yards ahead of Jim Hatfield. Bullets were flying about him. Hoarse yells, the shrieks of wounded rose in the chaparral.

It was difficult to distinguish the mixed-up groups of fighters. Confusion was fast getting the upper hand in the darkness.

Shoving through where the bush had been broken down by many hoofs, Hatfield came up behind a gathering bunch of A Bar O gunnies. They were forming themselves into a wedge under the roared commands of a couple of lieutenants, whose shrewder minds had realized what was up.

"Charge right through, boys," an A Bar O boss roared. "They're closin' the pincers. Shoot a hole in 'em!"

Head down, Hatfield spurred the golden flash around to the north flank. He cut west where the ranks of the A Bar O men were thin. His ready Colt blasted a reply to a challenging gunny. Bullets spat after him. But he smashed through to the other side of the line.

Now he saw before him dark shapes of more riders. He could make out the lighter patches of their faces, could even catch individual features in the flares of their guns.

"Barnes!" he cried. "It's Hatfield! Watch yore center. They're goin' to bust through."

"Hold it. Careful! That's the Ranger," Lew Barnes roared, spurring up. "Git down there, boys, hold 'em. Hard as hell to tell who's who out here," he shouted to Hatfield.

CHAPTER XVIII
THE REAL FOE

A terrible burst of shooting sounded to the south. Suddenly the flying wedge of gunnies raged forward and headed west, trying desperately to break the semi-circle and escape to the wilderness.

The yelling and gunfire increased in volume. Jim Hatfield spurred ahead, riding with mad abandon through the clutching chaparral.

The speed of the golden sorrel was thrilling. Wind in his face, dust whipped into clouds by hundreds of milling hoofs, the Ranger drove westward. He had to get in front of the juggernaut of destruction that was crashing through the strung-out line of cowboys and miners. Once through and started, there would be no way of stopping them. Then the mêlée would be complete.

He spurred south, certain he was out ahead. The dry leaves of the bush rattled in the stiff breeze. Cloud shadows scudded thick over the surface of the land.

Hatfield jumped from his leather, kneeled down, sheltering the match he cupped in one hand with his crouched body. Now that they had shot through the lines by main force of lead and hard riding, a horde of gunnies bore down on him. They had lost a lot of men, but fully half of the evil crew had made it. At their heels came Charlie Heidt and his cowboys, shooting after them. The guns snapped from side to side in the running battle.

A dry, thick stalk caught flame as the Ranger touched his fire to it. The wind wanted nothing better than this, and the wand of dried vegetation glowed bright red under its breath. He broke it off, held the improvised torch to the leaves of a withered bush. It flamed up instantly. Sparks danced in the breeze, catching the next bush. Hatfield ran on, the golden sorrel following him. He started another little conflagration, and a third, in the face of the approaching gunnies.

The wind whipped up the brush fire so swiftly that it was breath-taking. Only seconds elapsed from the time Hatfield lighted it until it was in full roar. Now the neighborhood was visible in a red blaze. Men could see whom they were fighting.

But the animals under them balked and shied from the flames.

Hatfield remounted. Gripping leather by long legs, he filled his guns with fresh lead. Behind the swift-running wall of smoke and fire he was in no danger of being burned. He was also hidden from the wedge of A Bar O killers.

Screams pierced through the roaring of guns and the crackle of the growing fire. No horse would ride into the flames. Smoke choked and blinded the hombres in front of it.

Jim Hatfield rode hell-for-leather to the upper limit of the fire he had started. So fast did the wind rush it toward the plaza of Eagleburg that there was only a little smoldering at the margins.

He headed back to the town. The gunnies, as well as Heidt's fighters and Lew Barnes' miners, were running before the brush conflagration. His swift action had prevented the escape of half the killers. . . .

Breaking out to the north of the plaza, he gazed down as he rode. There he saw the terrific mass of devils locked in struggle. Driven out by the Ranger onto the accurate guns of the deputies, who were ready and waiting for them, the gunnies had formed a ragged circle. Now they lashed back with full fury at Heidt and his men and the miners who sought to take them.

Coming to the cleared area, the fire had died off almost as quickly as it had begun, stopped by the bare dust of the yards and road. Smoke still drifted from the bush and from many exploding guns. But in the town lights the battle really took shape. Men could now tell whom they were shooting at.

Jim Hatfield spurred into the thick of the fray. His quick eyes swept the field. Horses were down. They rolled with their legs in the air. Their riders sprawled dead in the dirt or were wounded and crawling off, dragging punctured legs. Hate steamed to its full height that night in Eagleburg. Ranchers and miners, eager for vengeance on those who had so nearly destroyed them, fought against their real enemies, the gunnies of the A Bar O.

The Ranger searched for George Potter and Ted Morse but he had not seen the two chiefs. Nor did he see them now, in the midst of their fighting men.

"Ain't the kind to join this sort of fight," he muttered, as he went into action.

Formed by Barnes and Phelps, the semicircle ends had emerged before them, driving whatever gunnies the fire had missed. Unable to pass the rifles of the Ranger's placed deputies, the gunmen had bunched up for a last stand. Bullets were drilling into them. Hatfield charged, both Colts speaking. The terror inspired by the fury of the tall Ranger's attack flushed through evil hearts.

"The Ranger! The Ranger!"

Slugs whirled about him, tagging his clothes, biting his hide. But nothing could stop Hatfield. He rode the golden sorrel up and down, hunting the leaders, putting them out of action.

The uproar in Eagleburg was terrific. Women and the elderly kept to their homes, out of harm's way.

Goldy was nicked twice, bullets grooving his handsome hide. Charlie Heidt came roaring into Hatfield's vision. Shooting fast slugs into the seething mass of gunmen, Heidt was whooping it up, encouraging his men. Silent but efficient, Lew Barnes had his miners well in hand.

Closer whirled Jim Hatfield, Colts blazing. Death rode in Eagleburg that night — death to the evil faction that had terrorized the range across the Pecos.

"Throw down yore guns," bellowed the Ranger, "or we'll shoot down ev'ry one of yuh!"

Smashed by the Ranger's clever plan, their

attempt to bull through had been spoiled by his bush fire. Now the A Bar O men tried a final charge. Opposition was built up, hundreds of slugs tearing into the massed gunnies. Abruptly the charge stopped. They quailed before the fury of the Law as the tall Ranger rode forward on the golden sorrel. Men on the outskirts began throwing down their guns, raising their arms, begging for quarter.

A last, uneven volley came from the killers of the range. Three-quarters of them were hit, wounded or dead. Now the rest lost heart. They saw the silver star on silver circle gleaming on Jim Hatfield's vest, emblem of the Texas Rangers, and fear panicked them. More and more stopped shooting. Guns were flung to the dirt, and quavering voices cried for mercy.

"Hold it, gents!" roared Jim Hatfield, spurring in.

Quaking with fright, they knew they faced prison or even worse punishment for their awful crimes. The killers of the A Bar O watched the tall man on the golden sorrel, the hombre who had tracked them down and smashed them to the bitter end.

Hatfield wiped blood and dirt from his face. He swung on Lew Barnes as cowmen and miners crowded around their enemies, growling in savage fury that rose in threatening crescendo.

"S'pose we save the Law some dirty work, boys," a man yelled angrily. "Plenty of ropes around."

Jim Hatfield straightened in his saddle, his face lining in grim determination. He rode the sorrel along the line of prisoners, shunting back the men he had helped.

"Keep away, gents," he shouted. "No lynchin'. There's Ranger Law here!"

He signaled Lew Barnes, who trotted his horse up. The sheriff's face was caked with dirt and he had a nasty bullet hole in his left arm. But he was grinning with pleasure at the successful roundup of criminals.

"Lock these men up, Sheriff," commanded Hatfield. "I'll wanta question a couple of 'em."

He helped herd the prisoners into the jail. It bulged with them as deputies hustled to form a circle of guns about the building. Lew Barnes stood at the door with Jim Hatfield. They had dismounted when the captives were shoved inside.

Hatfield's cold eyes swept the gunnies. They could not face his gaze. He pointed to a couple of ratty looking devils he had crossed bullets with at the A Bar O and on the range.

"C'mere, you," he snapped ferociously, his eyes were icy glints. "Where's Potter?" he demanded as they were shoved, none too gently, toward him by Barnes. "No use to lie. The jig's up."

They were afraid of the tall Ranger and both hastened to reply, hoping to gain a little good will thereby.

"He done rode west, Mister Ranger," said the first quickly.

"Yeah, when he seen Al Osman was took, him'n Morse left in a hurry," agreed the second. "Left us to take the beatin', damn him."

Jim Hatfield nodded. "Figgered so," he muttered, swinging on his spurs.

He left the gunmen to Lew Barnes, who began checking them over, making sure there was no escape from the lockup.

Outside, panting men were tying up their wounds, wiping their hot, dusty faces. Many of them were starting for the saloons, for drink and food. The wind began to die down somewhat as dawn paled the sky.

Jim Hatfield stalked across the plaza, had a bite to eat and some hot coffee. He wanted another word with David Roberts. He located the Pecos Lady man in the Bull's Head. Roberts readily gave him the information he desired. . . .

At the crack of dawn Jim Hatfield made ready again to ride westward for the mountains. A dozen picked fighting men were equipped to accompany him in his pursuit of George Potter and Ted Morse. Potter, he was aware from his investigation, was the man whose evil brain had planned the devastation of the rangeland and the raid on the gold mine.

As he was saddling up a great dun-colored stallion, a magnificent animal John Carlton had insisted on lending the Ranger, the telegraph operator came hurrying to find him.

"Here's yore answer from Austin, Ranger."

Hatfield's gray-green eyes quickly scanned the message from Captain McDowell. It read:

Your man escaped six months ago. Wire if located.

A shrill whinny, half angry, half entreating, came from the open plaza. Hatfield turned as Goldy trotted up to him, bit angrily at the dun stallion Hatfield meant to ride west.

The Ranger petted the golden sorrel. Goldy was sadly scratched and bullet creases had scabbed on his handsome hide.

"Yuh're plumb wore out, Goldy," murmured Hatfield, arm around his mount's neck. "Stay here and rest. I'll be back."

Goldy didn't like it. Jerking back on the reins, kicking and bucking, he fought the wrangler from the livery stable who led him away.

Mounted on Carlton's beautiful dun stallion, Hatfield felt the tremendous spring of power under him. He signaled his posse and spurred westward in the graying light.

Chapter XIX
War to the Death

Before them loomed the rugged mountains where the Pecos Lady mine lay.

Wounds roughly bandaged, covered with alkali and matted with sweat from his hard ride, Jim Hatfield pushed the tiring, lathered dun stallion up the slope toward the mine. They had made the run from Eagleburg in remarkably fast time. Coming through Massacre Gap in the badlands, trail signs informed the keen-eyed Ranger how far in advance rode George Potter and Ted Morse.

He had stopped neither for wind, sun nor darkness. The sun was scintillatingly golden in his eyes as he crooned a song of encouragement to the fine animal carrying him. The dun's motion was not so smooth as Goldy's, but he had a great stride. The run as he had just made would have worn out any horse.

The tall Ranger was far ahead of the posse toiling behind him. It was strung out for miles according to the speed and endurance of their mounts, and the skill of the horsemen.

He skirted the deep crater that had been blasted out when the powder mine was touched off by the maddened David Roberts. Egged on by Potter and Morse, the man had believed he was defending his friends from murderous attackers.

On and on, toward the apparently deserted buildings, rode the Texas Ranger. The sun over the mountain top was blinding when he tried to seek the ridges with his eyes. The Pecos Lady seemed entirely abandoned. He saw the sluices still running as they had been left. Tools had been tossed here and there when the miners decided to retreat. The office door was still closed, and so were the portals of other buildings.

"They ain't so far ahead," he muttered to the dun. "Mebbe they've crossed the divide, though —"

Up to the northwest, from the scarred side of a crimson cliff dotted with coniferous trees, he saw a couple of birds flying off. His eyes narrowed. He turned that way, skirting past the office. As he came within a dozen yards of the building, he suddenly glimpsed the saddle horse ridden close to the smelting furnace.

He acted with the speed of light, threw himself sideways from his saddle. Clinging with his left hand to the horn, he balanced his weight on one stirrup. His right hand whipped out a blue-steel Colt to fire under the dun's arched neck. The big beast whirled over, rearing in the suddenness of the pivot.

Thrust through the office window, a rifle roared murderous bullets. The first clipped the top of his Stetson, ventilated it as he made his play. His eyes remained clear and unhurried by his narrow escape. He saw the splinters where his own hasty shot drilled a groove in the side of the window frame.

The second slug from the heavy rifle hit the dun in the breast, tore into his vitals. The big stallion sprang high into the air, ruining Hatfield's answering blast. Forced to disengage his spurred boot from the other stirrup, he just managed to get it clear as the great beast crashed in a heap to the rocky ground. The animal's weight hit the Ranger's ankle. A sharp pain stabbed up his leg.

Scrabbling in the rough stones, he fired from where he lay. A .30-30 slug cut through the flesh of his hip.

The blue-steel Colt, hot in his hand, contained only one more cartridge. He caught a glimpse of the bulbous-nosed, scarlet face of the rifleman in the office, who was eager to finish him off. With his teeth gritted against the anguish in his leg, he let go his final shot. He knew there would be no time to get out the second Colt that was pinned under his body.

The Winchester barrel still covered him. From that ominous black hole death would streak right at the officer, pinned under the dead weight of the dun.

Tugging at his leg, fighting to the last gasp, the Ranger sought to free himself. His boot was tight under the stallion. He tried to reach his spare Colt, but he could not twist enough to get it. Meanwhile, the seconds ticked off. The rifle still pointed at him, but it did not explode.

The shots had echoed through the craggy hills. Up to the pine-covered slope, a figure showed for an instant, staring down at the scene of death.

The instant lengthened into a minute as the pinned Ranger worked at his boot. His toes were numb but his whole leg hurt when he sought to contract his foot and draw it from the thick leather boot. He gave a last desperate yank. His leg came free of the circling cover!

The rifle continued to aim, but it was silent.

Bruised, hardly able to put any weight on his bare, bleeding leg, he pushed himself up. The skin was turning bluish. As he stood erect, drawing his second pistol, the blood rushing back into the limb felt like a thousand red-hot needles.

He hopped to the window. The barrel of the Winchester stayed frozen in position. He reached out. Easily he pulled it from where it rested on the sill. It was not held by Morse's hands.

Carefully he shoved the office door in with his pistol muzzle, peered through. Ted Morse, manager of the Pecos Lady, lay on his face under the window. There he had fallen, dropped by Hatfield's last .45 slug.

The sound of the big man's breathing was a horrible, gurgling gasp that was familiar to Hatfield. He had heard men with punctured lungs trying to suck in air.

A dim rifle explosion cracked on the keen, clear air of the mountains. There came the scream of a horse, close outside. Hatfield hopped to the window, looking west. Morse's saddled horse stood, jerking back his head, a hind leg painfully held up. A second bullet struck the animal. Hatfield saw the smoke puff from the upper slope.

He replied with six-gun bullets, but the

range was long for a revolver. He swore when he realized that George Potter had cut off quick pursuit. It might be hours before the posse came up. He could not even move save by limping, lurching hops.

Morse was groaning, but he was weakening fast. The Ranger dragged himself to the red-nosed hombre, Potter's chief lieutenant in the raid on the Pecos Lady.

Squatting by Morse, Hatfield stared into the pain-racked face of the dying manager.

"Yuh're handin' in yore checks, Morse," he rumbled. "Osman and his gunnies're captured. Yuh're through. Tell me where yuh met up with Potter and how yuh turned crooked. I savvy who he is."

The anguished eyes sought the steely orbs of the Ranger, dark with an icy light.

"You — you're a devil, Ranger! Damn him, he left me to face you alone!"

"Where's that gold him and you stole from the mine? Is it hid up there?"

Morse nodded. Like Al Osman, his fear of the Chief had now turned to hate in his dying moment.

"All of it — meant to use — to buy mine for a song —"

"Yuh had a dummy make that offer, didn't yuh? Some lawyer yuh enlisted. He sashayed fast when things busted open in Eagleburg.

Yuh didn't trust Al Osman to keep the gold."

"No — the Chief never would trust — anybody! Wanted to keep — gold where we — could get at it —"

"How'd yuh connect up with Potter?" demanded the Ranger. "He'd escaped from prison. I savvy why he hated John Carlton, the man who sent him there. Cimarron Jones, alias George Potter, didn't have no love for the man who sent him to jail!"

"So — yuh do know!" Grudging admiration lighted Morse's reddened eyes an instant, despite the fact that it was this tall Ranger who had shot him and ruined the plan of his chief. "Dunno — how you — found out — I'm the on'y one knew it here — Not even Osman could've told you —"

Jim Hatfield didn't take time to explain. The bit of wadding in the finger of the gantlet had inspired his wire to McDowell, asking the whereabouts of Cimarron Jones. The persecution of the Carltons had long puzzled him. Nor had he forgotten that Cimarron Jones had lost a fingertip in the gunfight with John Carlton in Kansas many years before.

Morse was willing to supply whatever information Hatfield needed to put all the pieces of the underground puzzle together.

His glance sought the whiskey bottle on the nearby table. Silently the Ranger reached for it, poured a big drink down the dying manager's gullet. It choked Morse. His eyes filled with water, but he was grateful for the fiery stuff.

"Potter — or Cimarron Jones, come down here jest to git even with Carlton?" asked Hatfield.

Morse shook his head. "No — he's too smart — for that. . . . I met Jones in prison — years back — served my time — Made a fresh start. Finally — got manager job here — Wrote Jones that Carlton was ranchin' across the Pecos — I'd heard the story. Jones escaped, months ago — Come to me for help — He had idea all the time of raidin' the mine. I know — he hated Carlton —

"But he feared Carlton'd recognize him sooner or later — Set up Osman's Syndicate to get rid of Carlton, clear range for use. . . . Fitted in perfect with revenge — He come here secretly — Got money from me — A letter to Elms in Austin, that got him job at the mine — We fooled Roberts with those painted bars — And Potter would never let the real — gold outa his — his —"

Blood spurted from Morse's throat. His neck seemed to lose all volition. His head sagged, and he died.

Jim Hatfield rose to his full height. He tried his bruised, strained leg. It held better, but he lurched heavily as he emerged from the office of the Pecos Lady.

Horseless, he swore. For far in the western distance he caught the glint of sunlight on metal. Cimarron Jones, alias George Potter, was on his way — headed for the Border!

Chapter XX
The Flash of Gold

Outside in the late afternoon light, with darkness threatening to fall over the mountains, Jim Hatfield stared eastward. He was hunting for a sign that his posse was coming up.

"Nuthin'," he muttered, impatiently.

Then, along the bushy, winding trail, he saw dust rising.

"One, anyways," he thought, watching the swift approach of the moving object below.

Another mile, and he exclaimed in amazement. A riderless, barebacked horse was flashing up the mountain toward him, running like a streak of hell.

"How'd that rascal git loose?" he grunted aloud.

Goldy, the Ranger's big sorrel, whinnied in glad greeting as he climbed up to his master's side. He stood shaking lather and dust off his thorn-scratched hide. He wore no saddle. The frayed ends of a hackamore showed how the sorrel had managed to break his rope and follow his master's trail. Goldy had had some rest. He had made the run from Eagleburg with no weight on him. Now he was in better condition than when Hatfield had left him behind. The sorrel nuzzled his hand.

"Yuh're shore a welcome sight, boy," Hatfield murmured as he pulled himself up on the golden flash's back. His injured leg stuck out stiffly from the heaving ribs of the horse.

An hour later, descending a steep ridge side, Jim Hatfield glimpsed the figure of Cimarron Jones in the dying light. The hombre was driving pack horses before him.

He was slowed by his determination to hang on to the fortune looted from the Pecos Lady. Desperately looking behind, Cimarron Jones saw the approaching Ranger drawing up inexorably.

He was trying to make the top of the next rise, but the unimpeded golden sorrel picked up yards on him. The muffled figure, bandanna up against dust, leaped from the back of his swift black. He grabbed off the rifle snugged in the sling.

"He's down," muttered Hatfield.

The shriek of the bullet close to them did not deter the officer's advance. Colt in hand, he began shooting at the murderous outlaw. Cimarron Jones had come back from living death to a gigantic raid on the decent folk of the Trans-Pecos.

Closer and closer came the Ranger. Cimarron Jones took a .45 slug through the shoulder. Hatfield saw him half spun around by the force of the bullet. The wide-faced devil dropped his Winchester and scuttled around the jagged rocks, out of sight.

Coming in, the Ranger knew it would mean certain death to swing that corner. Deadly fire was concentrated upon it by Cimarron Jones, the murderous hombre he had tracked to the end of the tether.

Hatfield slid off his pet sorrel, gave Goldy a caressing slap that sent the handsome horse back out of danger. His injured leg would hold little of his weight. But he could use one hand to support himself against the red boulder as he started around. His Colt was gripped and aimed up in his strong hand.

He unsnapped the strap that held his Stetson. He yanked the hat off, hung it on the end of his gun barrel. Carefully he stuck the hat out so that the ravening Cimarron Jones could glimpse it. Seeing it, the killer would think that Hatfield was trying to place him —

A vicious chunk of lead ripped the Stetson from his Colt. It twirled in the air as it sailed to the rocky trail, punctured in the center. Had the tall Ranger's head been inside, it would have been an instantly fatal shot, through the brain.

The echoings of the explosion rattled in the steep rocks. But an instant-fraction after Jones had fired, Hatfield leaped from his crouch, propelled by his good leg to the corner. Taking advantage of the momentary pause after the other's shot, Hatfield fired twice before falling back behind his cover, away from Jones' reply.

"He's shore holed up in there," he muttered.

He wiped dust from his eyes. His face had been stung by flying fragments of stone that sprayed under his foe's striking slugs. He had seen the flare of Cimarron Jones' Colt, in the mouth of a cave to the right, a few yards around the bend. The shrewd outlaw was well-hidden from Hatfield's return fire.

Trying again, the Ranger aimed at the spot where he glimpsed blue-red ribbons of flame in the cavern's maw. Powder flashes drove heavy bullets his way. But he heard the slaps of his slugs on rock. Then he knew that Jones shifted after each volley he let go.

"He ain't hurt so bad, that's plain," muttered the officer.

He was slow in leaping back after aiming at the gun spurts in the deep shadows. He felt a hot slug slice viciously through his hair. Blood spurted from the gashed scalp.

Cool as though out for a stroll in the hills, the tall Ranger figured the odds. This duel wasn't going the Law's way. Inside the cavern, Jones commanded the turn and the approach to the mouth of the hole in the rocks. He stood a good chance of plugging Hatfield before the Ranger could locate his target.

"Hafta try it diff'rent," mused Hatfield. Even if he waited till night actually fell, Jones would still be able to see him against the lighter sky, hear him as he came stalking him across the rocks.

He glanced up. His unhurried gaze examined the immediate terrain. In the red cliff were steep shelves over his head. He figured he could use them for steps, with a little pulling help from his arms. A bulging lip above would cover him until he got up close to the mouth of the cave. . . .

The sun dropped behind the western mountains. A wind whined across the dry reaches of the Trans-Pecos, rattling the mesquite pods, coating everything with alkali dust. Night came as Hatfield began climbing, pulling himself up with his arms, shoving with his good leg. At all times, though, he carefully kept close against the cliff.

He had to have his guns holstered for this work. Once he slipped, he would roll right down into Jones' guns. Twice his foe let go a shot, evidently trying to draw out the Ranger and find out where he was. Cimarron Jones hoped he had really got his Nemesis, the man who had driven him into the open. . . .

"Fight, you Ranger coyote!" Jones shrieked.

Hatfield was beginning to cross over now. He crawled along a narrow rock ledge that slanted downward. It would take him directly above the mouth of the cavern.

The soft darkness was like a blanket on the wilderness. Stars twinkled in the winey air, and the moon was just a glow on the horizon, for it had not yet risen.

Cimarron Jones was growing apprehensive about the Ranger's position. He shot again, hoping to draw an answer. Hatfield hung to the side of the cliff. His left hand gripped a jutting rock. Cautiously he was working his Colt from the holster with his right.

The cliff was eroded. In the night it was impossible to check on handholds and footing. A chunk of rock dislodged under the Ranger's weight, crashed down in front of the cavern. Instantly Cimarron Jones knew what the Ranger's game was.

"So that's your play," snarled Jones. "You'll never take me, Ranger!"

Catching himself with his hand, Hatfield was close to Jones.

"Come out, Jones! Come out or I'll come in after yuh!"

A laugh that was fury incarnate was his reply. Colt gripped in hand, gray-green eyes shining, he let go. Sliding down the dark face of the rocks, Hatfield landed in a crouched position. He did not stop his motion but whipped his lithe body around. He rolled inward as a gun flash lighted the cave. He seized a glimpse of the twisted, frenzied face of his arch-enemy. Blood showed on Cimarron Jones — blood from Ranger lead!

Hatfield's Colt roared. Bullets spattered against the rock behind Jones. Always shifting in at his foe, Hatfield scrabbled forward. He never thought of retreat.

Confusion shrieked in the confines of the cavern. A slug bit Hatfield's cheek, grooved it with a bloody gash. Another slashed through his leg calf, cutting a chunk from his boot-top. But the Ranger disappeared inside the black cave. Fierce as a wildcat at bay, armed with pistols, Cimarron Jones fell back before the fury of Hatfield's onslaught.

The terrific power of the Ranger's attack appalled Cimarron Jones, shook his aim. His Colt faltered as Hatfield hunted him in the blackness. Jones turned, ran back into the winding cavern. Hatfield did not know how deep it reached into the mountain.

He paused to listen, heard the hurried footsteps echoing inside. He started after Jones, shooting as he came, zigzagging to prevent his man from aiming at his gun-flash.

Jones stopped at a turn, hastily sent two quick ones at him. Hatfield felt the wind of them past his cheek. He clipped the rocks, spraying lead and bits of stone into Jones' eyes.

Up again from his shooting crouch, Jim Hatfield plunged on. He felt his way with a hand and each foot, lurching heavily on his injured leg.

The air grew staler and warm in the recesses of the cavern, as it wound down into the mountainside. He heard the splash of water ahead and the muttered cursing of his foe.

"Throw out yore guns, I tell yuh," Hatfield ordered, an icy threat in his strong voice.

"Here, damn you! Take it! You asked for it
—"

A big pistol crashed into his face, cutting
the flesh, bruising his nose. Cimarron Jones
had flung an empty gun at him. The whirling weapon had caught Hatfield as he
charged.

Rapidly the Ranger swung the next curve.
Water suddenly splashed up over his boots.
He stood in a knee-deep pool that was
absolutely undisturbed by wind inside the
cave. It was clear as crystal. Ahead, Cimarron Jones was wading. Underground springs
fed this little lake. It ran out through
crevices below, to join the rushing torrent
that fed the sluices of the hydraulic miners.

"Reckon he's got another gun," muttered
Hatfield.

His eyes stung. His ears rang madly from
the explosions of big pistols in that confined
space. But he could not have used his eyes
in progressing, for the blackness was like
pitch.

Gun clenched in one hand, his left arm
stretched out to touch the clammy cave
wall, Hatfield cautiously but relentlessly
pursued.

Cimarron Jones muttered a hoarse curse
that echoed like the whisper of a ghoul in
the tense silence of the cave. A heavy, furry

body blindly slapped the Ranger's face. He heard the whirring of wings as a great bat, disturbed by the intruders, left its perch and flew toward the outer air.

A second bat brushed him. About his head came a whole bunch of them, flying outward. Heavy splashings ahead told his keen ears that Cimarron Jones had gone into deeper water. He paused, listening intently.

He stuck out his wounded leg, stirred the water to one side with his boot. The sudden flash of a gun showed that the chamber opened wide in here. A huge underground lake occupied the lower reaches of the caverns. Stalactites hung from above. The blinding light from Cimarron Jones' other Colt scared an army of fat bats into frantic escape.

Up to his waist in the cool, inky water, stood Cimarron Jones. He could go no farther and still keep his footing. His slug struck the water with a plugging, throaty sound. Hatfield let go a shot, instantly crouching down. Water cooled him, washed his wounds.

"Yuh're done, Jones," he stated calmly.

Cimarron Jones didn't fancy a return to the prison he had escaped. His bullets sought the oncoming Ranger. But the man's nerve was slipping. His aim was no longer so steady. He was appalled by the fighting strength and inexorable courage of Jim Hatfield.

"One — two —" Hatfield was counting the gun shots, as he drew the hombre's fire. Always working closer, he crouched down low in the water, bobbing up to shoot, then swiftly falling aside.

"Three — four — five —"

Hatfield shoved off from the side of the cave wall. He lunged at Jones, trapped between the Ranger and deep water.

Chapter XXI
Payment in Lead

By hearing, Hatfield sensed his foe's position as Jones sought to elude his reaching hand. Cursing, Cimarron Jones lashed out with his gun barrel. The sharp sight stabbed at the Ranger. Hatfield's injured leg gave way under him when he stubbed against the rock. But as he fell he had one hand on Jones. He dragged down the hombre with him.

It was like holding to a fighting grizzly. Jones was insane with rage. He scratched, bit and kicked, trying to get Hatfield by the throat. Hatfield wrested his second gun away from him. The two men locked close, rolling under water, then struggling up, seeking vital air.

Half drowned, Hatfield kept a grip on Cimarron Jones. They hit the rocky bottom, slippery with ooze. The noises of the struggle echoed in the cavern like two roaring monsters fighting for supremacy.

Cimarron Jones seemed far from through. He got a sharp-nailed hand into Hatfield's face, gouged the Ranger's eyes. Venomously he brought up his knees, shoved hard, and flipped back. Hatfield's spine cracked agonizingly against the sharp outcropping of rock on the bottom. His boot slid in the muck as he forced himself to the surface and drew in air.

For a moment he stood in the depth to his armpits. Then he heard Cimarron Jones, off to his right, splashing through shallower water. He had lost his orientation in the twisting and turning under the surface. Starting forward at the sound of his enemy, a sudden stab of bluish flame blinded him. Something hot bit into his chest muscles, under his left arm.

"Damn him — Got a pocket gun," he muttered.

The shock of the smaller-caliber slug stopped him. He staggered, nearly went under for good, as he groped for his holstered Colt. By the volume of fire from Jones' shot and the bang he guessed the size of the pistol. Jones had probably held it in a shoulder holster under his shirt, until his .45's were emptied. Such hombres often toted as many as four pistols.

The .32 did not stop Jim Hatfield, but it

was the worst wound he had yet received. Dangerously shocking, it had come close to his vitals. He had to use every ounce of his fighting power to keep from collapse, to stay on the trail of Cimarron Jones. Recovery took him moments that dragged like hours. Breath rasped in his great lungs. He fought to free the Colt from its pleated leather case. His painful struggle was nothing like that of the fastest draw west of New Orleans.

Once again the sinister, slippery Cimarron Jones sensed that victory over the Ranger was within his grasp. He raised the small gun he had cleverly kept in reserve.

"Another puncture like that last one," Hatfield thought, "and —"

His leg was numb. It kept giving under him. He had to catch all his weight on his other foot, splashing madly for balance. Jones easily placed him as he staggered forward. The .32 barked. The stab of powder flame flashed lurid in the black. Echoes snapped back and forth, insane in their confinement. The slug whistled within an inch of the Ranger's ear.

Hatfield raised his thumb off the Colt hammer. The firing-pin of the .45 struck home to the rim. Exploded powder drove the big slug straight at the heart of Cimarron Jones' fire. There hadn't been an instant's pause. It was as though the echo were greater than the sound. . . .

Teetering on his good leg, Hatfield shook his head, fighting to clear it. But the terrific strain of fighting suddenly flushed his brain with blackness. He collapsed in waist-deep water. His head went under.

Submersion, the cry of his lungs for air, shocked him back to consciousness. He came up to the surface, weaving toward the draught blowing from the opening of the cave mouth. He fell again, pushed himself on with his arms. Suddenly, he could not tell how, he was out of the water, creeping blindly on the dry rubble of the cavern floor.

He crawled on hands and knees a few feet before he collapsed. He had no idea how long he had been there when he regained consciousness.

He sat up, shaking his racked, pounding head. He was no longer sopping.

"Huh — Musta been — out a long while —"

It was quiet as a tomb in the cave. His matches were damp, ruined. His shirt and pants clung soggily to him and his boots were wet. His feet sloshed as he limped around.

Catching himself after regaining his wind, he began hunting in the darkness for Cimarron Jones.

He found his enemy after a few minutes. The body lay on the bottom, in three feet of water. He bumped against it as he cut back and forth across the cavern, feeling with his feet.

He got hold of the dead man's shirt collar, dragged the corpse of Cimarron Jones along the cave, up to the mouth. A gibbous moon hung over the great mountains. Its silvery light glowed on the wind-rustled growth. Rock spires cast purple-black shadows in its path.

Hatfield stepped from the ebony, irregular patch that was the cavern's maw. Cimarron Jones dragged stiff and horizontal behind him. The Ranger's last bullet had drilled the evil brain of the arch-criminal who had brought six-gun fury and the horror of wholesale slaughter across the Pecos.

He stood, taking in deep breaths of the keen air. Unsteady on his feet, he braced himself with a hand against the cliff, and whistled. Instantly a golden shape whinnied, came trotting up to him.

"One tough sidewinder, Goldy," Hatfield muttered. The sorrel nuzzled his hand, sniffed inquiringly at the blood his keen nose smelled. "That's 'bout as close as yuh could come without goin' all the way!

Thanks to you, we got him."

Jim Hatfield, Texas Ranger, wiped grime from his brow. He cleaned his eyes with his damp bandanna. It was a difficult chore for him, usually so powerful, to hoist the dank body of Cimarron Jones to Goldy's back. He let it ride behind him, head on one side of the horse, legs limply dangling on the other.

He picked up the pack animals that Cimarron Jones had brought up this far, before Hatfield overtook him and prevented his escape.

Driving the laden horses ahead of him, the Ranger headed back toward the Pecos Lady. A fire glowed red against the mountainside, near the office, when Hatfield walked the sorrel up into the circle of light. His gray-green eyes sought the figures of the men who jumped up at sound of his approach. Shorty Olliphant was here, and other deputies who had trailed him out from Eagleburg.

"Hey, Ranger!" cried Shorty, giving a whoop of pleasure. It had taken him a full minute to recognize the bedraggled hombre on the sorrel. "There yuh are! Where yuh been, huh?"

"To hell and back," Hatfield told him dryly. "Say, corral them pack horses, Shorty.

236

Make it pronto. Me, I'd like a cup of coffee."

Stiffly he dismounted, limped over and sat down on a wooden box in the circle of firelight. Dusty and tired from their long drive, the deputies had run their horses ragged. They had paused to catch their breath at the office and lighted this fire to cook some food. A lamp in the office shone on the stiffened corpse of Ted Morse. The men stared with amazement at the battered Ranger, then at the dead Cimarron Jones. The bullet hole between his glazed eyes was blue now.

"Whew!" gasped Olliphant. "That musta been some trip, Mister Big Jigger!"

Willing hands aided him, carried out the Ranger's commands. Expert riders brought in the pack horses. At Hatfield's order, Shorty slit one of the packs balanced at either side. The canvas loads had been lashed with diamond hitches. The firelight suddenly gleamed on yellow metal.

"Gold!" cried Shorty.

"That's it." Hatfield nodded. "That's the gold stolen from the Pecos Lady, gents. It never did leave here. Morse and Cimarron Jones kept it hid up above and sent out fake stuff to fool Roberts and the others."

■ ■ ■ ■

Days later, Jim Hatfield still walked with a limp. His tough hide was seamed with healing bullet scars. He stepped into Captain Bill McDowell's office in Austin, Texas.

McDowell sprang up, grasped his star's hand, grinning as he pumped the tall Ranger's arm.

"Yuh cleared it, doggone if yuh didn't, Jim! Saved the range and the Pecos Lady folks too. Nobody but you could've brought it off!"

But the Captain's seamed, red face grew grave as he took in the scars of bullets, the tautness of the skin stretched over the man's cheek-bones. The trifling fat had slewed off Jim Hatfield in his terrific ordeal across the Pecos.

"Sit down, man," McDowell ordered. Hatfield's wide mouth turned up at the corners, amused by his superior's solicitude. "Here, have a cigar. Have a drink. Yuh need it."

McDowell cleared his throat, frowning as he resumed his seat behind his desk. He rustled the telegram he had received from Hatfield before the Ranger had left Eagleburg. It was Hatfield's only written report, and it consisted of the following terse sentence:

HAVE SETTLED TROUBLE AND RECOVERED GOLD HATFIELD

"Yuh shore don't waste words," snapped McDowell. "If Sheriff Lew Barnes was as stingy with County money as you are with the State's, I'd never savvy anything, Jim. This here Cimarron Jones was a right clever devil. But yuh walked right in and fit him to a finish in a mountain cave and brought him out. But not alive, the way John Carlton done it in Kansas."

Hatfield shrugged. "He wouldn't surrender, Cap'n. Reckon he didn't cotton to another stay in prison, even if he beat the noose. It was sorta dark in that cavern, and I couldn't pick my spot at the end — I'd've been back yesterday, but they made me stay for a weddin'. Carlton's son got hitched to Elsie Wills, a neighbor gal."

"So the range is clear. Yuh made peace 'tween miners and cowmen, Barnes says. I'm glad. They're most of 'em good citizens on both sides. Elms claims the Pecos Lady company 'll be okay, what with the gold yuh recovered. What was this 'bout Cimarron Jones sendin' out painted iron blocks 'stead of the real metal?"

"That was to fool David Roberts, for one thing. Roberts is an honest man. Morse kept him busy while Jones done the switchin', hidin' the real gold in a cave in the hills. Then Jones didn't trust Al Osman any too far, and he was right at that. He wanted that gold where he could git it himself. He was too smart to go right after John Carlton direct. But he hadda git rid of him for fear Carlton would recognize him 'spite the weight he'd put on, his beard and dyed hair. His revenge on Carlton fitted in perfect with his plans to take control over the mine and the range across the Pecos."

A sharp tap on the outer door brought a frown of annoyance to McDowell's accordion-pleated brow.

"Now what the hell d' yuh want?" he roared at the scared looking clerk who stuck his head in the door, blinking as the boss yelled at him.

" 'Scuse me, Cap'n McDowell — I hate to bother yuh — But a wire jest come in from the Big Bend country, Brewster way . . . Sheriff there claims Ranger Ned Volten was caught in the Bearcat Saloon by twelve outlaws. He stepped in outa the bright sunlight and was sorta blinded. He on'y got three of 'em 'fore they kilt him —

240

Sheriff says he looked like a flour sieve —"

McDowell leaped to his feet, cursing.

"Is Ranger Thomas back yet?" he shouted furiously.

"No, sir. Nobody's around at the moment."

"I'm around," murmured Jim Hatfield, pulling himself to his feet, facing his grizzled chief.

McDowell stared at him, at the marks of the recent terrific struggles across the Pecos.

"No, no! I can't ask yuh to ride so soon again, Jim. It would mebbe finish yuh — Yuh're wounded and lame. Yuh got to have a rest. Yuh —"

Fifteen minutes later McDowell stood outside Ranger Headquarters, staring westward. Jim Hatfield was riding off, carrying Ranger Law to the Texas Frontier.

We hope you have enjoyed this Large Print book. Other Thorndike, Wheeler, and Chivers Press Large Print books are available at your library or directly from the publishers.

For information about current and upcoming titles, please call or write, without obligation, to:

Publisher
Thorndike Press
295 Kennedy Memorial Drive
Waterville, ME 04901
Tel. (800) 223-1244

or visit our Web site at:

http://gale.cengage.com/thorndike

OR

Chivers Large Print
published by BBC Audiobooks Ltd
St James House, The Square
Lower Bristol Road
Bath BA2 3SB
England
Tel. +44(0) 800 136919
email: bbcaudiobooks@bbc.co.uk
www.bbcaudiobooks.co.uk

All our Large Print titles are designed for easy reading, and all our books are made to last.